THE HORROR FILM KILLER

THESE KIDS ARE DYING
TO FINISH THEIR FILM

A FILM MILIEU THRILLER

MICHAEL J. BOWLER

The Horror Film Killer
(A Film Milieu Thriller)
Copyright © 2021 by Michael J. Bowler
All rights reserved.
First Edition: 2021

Paperback ISBN: 978-1-7333290-3-3
Hardcover ISBN: 979-8-9862241-9-0
eBook ISBN: 978-1-7333290-4-0

Editor: Loretta Sylvestre
Cover and Formatting: Streetlight Graphics

CHAPTER ONE

THE FIRST MURDER

Tony staggers and nearly topples before reaching the park bench and collapsing into a seated position. His backpack leaks random food wrappers from a ragged gash up the side and his shoulders slump so sharply he nearly tumbles to the grass at his feet. Exhausted and barely able to stay upright, he lies back the bench and within moments falls into a deep sleep.

Wind kicks up leaves around the bench, and thick shade trees obscure most of the illumination cast by the nearest streetlight. The park is empty, the adjacent street devoid of movement, and no city sounds penetrate this deep in the suburbs.

Tony slumbers on, arms draped across his chest as though he's posing for the part of a corpse in some murder mystery. Shadows surround him, shifting in the meager light, trembling in the wind.

Tony's face is twisted with pain, yet serene, as though this minor respite is the best thing that's happened to him all day. He doesn't look more than twenty-three or four, but the ravages of street life have taken their toll, and he could easily pass for thirty-four if given a cursory inspection.

So sudden it's almost too fast to follow, a gloved hand shoots out from under the bench from beneath and clamps down on Tony's mouth. His eyelids flip open like window shades and the whites glow bright with shock. Before he can even struggle, the sharp tip of an arrow exits his throat from beneath, tearing through the skin with a sound like ripping cloth.

Blood erupts from his trachea as his eyes bug out in anguish and stunned horror. His mouth opens and closes like a fish out of water as the tip of the arrow dribbles dark red blood into a rapidly growing pool, spilling through the slats of the wooden bench beneath him. He twists and flops, but the hand keeps his forehead pinned to the bench until all movement stops and his mouth ceases its desperate attempts to suck in air. The eyes remain open, the pupils etched with terror and disbelief. Slowly, the gloved hand slips off his face and vanishes beneath the bench. The metal spear remains in place, blood bubbling from the jagged flesh around it like lava from a volcano.

Footsteps run away and Tony remains pinned to the bench, finally at peace.

"Cut!" Ashley leans away from the monitor and applauds with gusto. "That's a wrap for tonight, everyone. It looked fantastic!"

The teen who's been filming lowers his camera as the twenty-something actor on the bench sits up and grins.

"Somebody help Grant get that arrow out of his throat," Ashley adds with a laugh.

Grant chuckles as several teen crew members scurry over and set about removing the apparatus that encircles his neck.

"This Karo syrup is nasty, Ashley," Grant says, twisting his face into a grimace. "And cold, too."

Ashley saunters over. "What, you expect me to heat it up for you? You're just an expendable extra so get over yourself."

He sticks out his tongue and she laughs.

The image freezes and then goes black.

"Okay, I'm going to stop here since the bell's about to ring."

Bright light fills the room as Mr. Ketchum flicks on the overheads. Cassie beams with pride as the class of high school seniors applauds. A bank of open windows opposite the door allows a slight breeze to waft through the room, partially offsetting the warm spring temperature outside.

On the white board behind Mr. Ketchum's desk is scrawled in large red letters, *HAPPY FRIDAY THE 13*[TH]. Also, in the upper right corner are the words Filming Always Permitted in this Classroom, and beneath that two signatures—*Mr.* K and Mrs. K.

Cassie flips an errant strand of auburn hair off her freckled face and tosses Donovan a smile of triumph. That sequence, including the kill, was lensed just last weekend, which means they spent long hours in the school's editing room to have it ready for today. Watching that particular murder on Friday the 13th is especially delicious since the "kill" is an homage to that very movie.

The applause dies down as Kristen Corte, playing "Ashley" in the film, stands and bows. "Thank you, thank you."

Two rows over, attractive brunette Olivia Taylor scowls. "We're clapping for the kill scene, not *you*, Kristen."

Kristen loses her gloating smile. "I keep hoping they'll rewrite the script and kill you off sooner."

Mr. Ketchum holds up a hand. "Enough behind the scenes drama, ladies." He sends each of the girls a serious look that says, "I mean business here," and they back down. Kristen retakes her seat and grabs Diego Bernal's hand, pulling him closer and mad-dogging Olivia.

Cassie sighs to herself. Another typical day in film class. Kristen and Olivia are probably the prettiest girls at school, and that's the problem. Cassie doesn't care enough about stuff like that to be jealous, but the other two girls are so much alike they can't stand one another.

Blonde hair tumbling past her shoulders, small nose, blue eyes, soft features, and a figure to kill for, Kristen is eye candy for every boy who sees her. Olivia is almost the opposite with short brown hair, sharp features, and piercing brown eyes, but her flirting skills are legendary and could easily give Kristen a run for her money if Kristen ever broke up with Diego, her steady boyfriend of the past two years.

"I, for one, am very impressed," Mr. Ketchum goes on, turning his attention Cassie's way. "Your footage looks professional. The lighting and camerawork—great job, William."

Tall, skinny William Webster grins from ear to ear from behind long bangs swept across light brown eyes, his barely visible mustache stretched to pencil thin status.

"And that opening drone shot as the victim staggered into the park and plopped onto the bench was flawless," Mr. Ketchum goes on, his deep voice filled with pride. "Your precision with that drone astonishes me, Baxter. I can't even keep one of those things in the air for two minutes without crashing it into something."

Baxter Jacobs—known as the class nerd for his large glasses and pudgy physique—basks in the glow of the compliment, lowering his eyes in embarrassed pride.

"Your sound was clean too, Baxter," Mr. Ketchum adds. "That's very difficult during location shooting." He scans the class. "Any comments or suggestions for the directors, cast, or crew before we leave for spring break?"

Cassie's least-favorite classmate, Robert Wilkins, leers at her. "Gonna tell us who the killer is, Cass?"

"Not on your life. Not even the main actors have seen those pages."

"I'm the only one privileged to know that secret." Mr. Ketchum grins and pulls an imaginary zipper across his lips. "But my lips are sealed under penalty of death."

The class laughs.

"I'm sure it was Cassie who threatened you." Robert smirks. "We all know Donovan's too feeble to intimidate a fly."

"Ahem!" Mr. Ketchum tosses a ball painted with a frown face to Robert, who deftly plucks it from the air it with his left hand. He eyes the frowning face and shrugs.

"Sorry, Mr. K, but it's true."

Mr. Ketchum is not amused. "If you end up with Mr. Frown one more time, Robert, I'll dock you some serious class participation points."

Robert looks suitably chastised, but Cassie tosses him the dirtiest look she can muster. Tall, dark-haired, handsome, and narcissistic to the max, Robert loves displaying his chiseled physique at every opportunity. Today, he's wearing shorts and skin-tight tank top that might as well be invisible.

Cassie hates arrogance, especially when people flaunt it. Robert has haughtily hit on her multiple times this year, clearly assuming his charm and hot bod are all he needs to conquer her.

Considering he could have practically any girl at school, she doesn't understand his persistence—unless he considers her a challenge. She's turned him down as forcefully as possible and, in his self-absorbed mind, Robert assumes it's because of Donovan.

Donovan lowers his eyes to the floor under the scrutiny of the class. A shadow from his yellow fedora covers his face and gives him a tragic-figure look that sends Cassie's heartbeat into raging overdrive.

How dare Robert!

She bites her lip, fighting the urge to cuss him out right then and there!

"Even I'm not privileged to know the identity of the killer," comes a husky female voice from the back of the room. "And I'm married to the producer." She tosses off a throaty laugh and the class chuckles.

"What did you think of my performance, Mrs. K?" Kristen chirps, her tone indicating she expects a compliment. "Do you think I might play Lady Macbeth one day like you did?"

Mrs. Ketchum, the school's acting teacher, brushes a loose strand of brown hair back over one ear and appears to consider the question.

"I know you've always fancied that performance of mine and I confess I'm rather proud of it. But sometimes I fear you aspire to be like Lady Macbeth in real life."

"Of course, I do," Kristen asserts in her usual take-no-prisoners tone. "She was a take-charge woman, the kind you've modeled for us."

"May I point out," Mr. K adds, "that she was also an accessory to murder. But we're getting sidetracked here."

"I'm proud of every one of you," Mrs. K announces in her most dramatic tone. "The performances are stellar, especially you, Kristen. You are, after all, playing against type as a nice girl, am I right?"

She smiles and everyone joins her, including Kristen, who may be self-absorbed and conceited, but at least makes no pretense of being otherwise.

Cassie has always considered Mrs. K one of the most beautiful women she's ever known, possessing true movie star attributes. Brunette with shoulder-length, wavy hair swept just off the face, full lips accented by understated lipstick, lovely green eyes beneath luxuriously long lashes. Even her high cheekbones give her that star quality, like a modern-day version of Sophia Loren.

Mr. and Mrs. K used to be active in Hollywood—he a director and she an actress—but drinking, drugs, and partying derailed both their careers. They've never tried to keep their pasts a secret—Google has all the dirty details—and Mr. K, at least, has always asserted that he loves teaching more than directing any day. Cassie can't imagine that being true, but she doesn't argue the point.

Mrs. Ketchum looks across the room at Cassie and Donovan. "You two are going places in Hollywood, I've no doubt of that. Perhaps you can convince my husband to produce your next feature."

Cassie's mouth drops open. "Are you thinking of going back to making movies, Mr. K? That would be awesome!"

Dressed in his usual sloppy wrinkled pants and long-sleeved pullover, Mr. Ketchum looks nothing like how she pictures a Hollywood producer.

"That's just my wife's wishful thinking. I prefer nurturing the talent in this room. You and Donovan will do just fine on your own. I agree with Mrs. K on that score."

He nods at his wife and she smiles back. But something about the smile seems off to Cassie, as though Mrs. K thinks Mr. K embarrassed her in front of the students.

"I, uh, I agree about Donovan and Cassie," pipes up a timid voice from the back corner. "It's an honor to work with them."

Cassie turns toward the back of the class.

Jaden Merton slouches in his usual seat, black hoodie partially covering his perfectly woven cornrows, peeking out at them as though afraid he'll be attacked at any moment.

Donovan smiles at the compliment. "Thanks, man," he says in that calm, quiet tone that's soothed Cassie's bull-in-a-china-shop nature since they were children. "You're a great help on the set, and I mean that. You have, like, a photographic memory for details."

Jaden cracks what for him could pass for a smile, but he doesn't respond to the compliment. He seldom says anything at all, but the film crew would be minus its most valuable member if he decided to quit.

It had taken Cassie and Donovan more than a few pleading sessions before Mr. Ketchum agreed to let them co-write and co-direct a feature film for their senior project. Everyone else is making short films, but Cassie and Donovan hope to enter their movie in the local Shriek Festival, one of the oldest and biggest horror film festivals in the country. Final deadline for submissions is in July. Since their film has to be finished and polished before the June graduation date, submitting on time should be a breeze. And they both live in the San Fernando Valley, so attending the nearby Hollywood-based festival will be a cinch.

Mr. Ketchum studies Jaden a long moment, but the lanky African American boy refuses to make eye contact.

"I've heard good things about your work on this film, Jaden, and I'm happy to see you enjoying yourself."

"He enjoys himself too much," Kristen spits out, squinting at Jaden from across the room. "He gets a little too into his role as the guy in the skull mask."

"He's the killer?" a longhaired girl exclaims in shock.

Mr. Ketchum shakes his head. "He's the body double for the killer. That way, none of the other actors know which character is really doing the killing."

The girl nods in admiration.

Jaden withers beneath Kristen's verbal assault.

"Kristen," Mr. Ketchum intones, his voice sounding as annoyed as Cassie has ever heard from him. "I agreed to you not having to make your own film because you're the lead in this one. Don't push me. If I get reports that you're playing the prima donna on set like you do here, you'd better come up with an Oscar-caliber film of your own if you want to pass this class."

Olivia bursts into applause, and surprisingly Jaden joins her. Now it's Kristen who withers—slightly—and Cassie is pleased to note that she doesn't argue or even respond. She merely pulls Diego in closer and he whispers something—no doubt words of comfort—into her ear. That's all he ever seems to do.

Diego Bernal has been called the hottest boy at Performance Arts Academy High School by most of the girls Cassie knows. She agrees that he has that smoldering Latino look and he could easily be a model with his wavy black hair, smooth features untarnished by acne or beard stubble, and soft brown eyes. But he's not her type. He's too... beautiful.

One thing she *does* know—he could do a helluva lot better in the girl-friend department that Kristen Corte. Cassie can't imagine what he sees in her beyond beauty. That must be all he wants.

Kristen is practically a Hollywood stereotype, the obnoxious drama queen everyone hates. That's why it was too tempting to pass up the opportunity to cast her as the "good girl" in this film. She's not joking when she crows about being a great actress. She really is stellar and will no doubt have the Hollywood career she craves if she can keep her attitude in check.

Mr. Ketchum continues the discussion for a few more minutes and then quizzes other class members about the status of their scripts or film projects.

Cassie tunes out to think about the week ahead. She and Donovan have lined up some pretty cool locations and the weather promises to be clear. Since it's already April, Daylight Savings Time is in play. That means longer days, but also a longer wait for night shooting to begin. They've discussed the schedule so often they have it memorized, and plan on making the best use of every shooting moment they have.

When Mr. Ketchum dismisses the class, Cassie gathers up her backpack and smiles as Donovan assembles his stuff. The class files out, several students wishing them success on the rest of the shoot.

Asher, the smallest boy in the senior class despite having just turned eighteen is, in Cassie's opinion, one of the cutest boys in the entire school. He's around five foot five, with a 'fro of thick curly brown hair that wraps itself around his head like a Chia pet, pale blue eyes the color of Forget-Me-Not flowers, and soft, delicate features that make him look much younger.

"See you tomorrow, Cassie," he says in his typically upbeat voice as he passes her desk.

"Yep." She smiles at him as he leaves the room.

Asher volunteered for the cameraman role in the film because he looks up to William, who also aspires to be a Director of Photography after high school. Cassie loves having Asher on set for two reasons: he's one of the nicest kids around and he's gorgeous. Even in a small role, he'll be additional eye candy to lure in female viewers. Cassie is feminist to a point, but recognizes the usefulness of having good-looking people, both male and female, in a film. That's just good business.

She glances around for Jaden, but he was likely the first one out, as always. Jaden isn't like Asher and, if Cassie is honest, he creeps her out a little. He gives new meaning to the word "shy"; he stares a lot and doesn't talk. More than once in class—and now on set—she's felt his eyes fixed on her, or maybe on her and Donovan together.

Could he be jealous of Donovan? She's never seen him show interest in anyone and she isn't exactly the prettiest or most interesting girl on campus with her frizzy auburn hair and brown freckles littering her face like specks of dust. Still, for a timid kid like Jaden, a whirling dervish of energy might seem alluring. With her, he'd never have to talk, just listen.

"Ready?" Donovan is standing beside her, his military green backpack slung over one shoulder, completely at color odds with his mismatched clothes. Cassie loves that he buys everything from thrift stores and then puts on whatever he finds in his closet without bothering to match styles or colors.

Today his red-checkered flannel shirt completely misses the mark against his green and black striped long pants and the yellow fedora resting an angle atop a mop of messy brown hair sticking out from underneath like he's an anime character.

She always describes him as "cute" because of those hazel eyes set beneath perfect brows that most girls would kill for and his dimpled smile, which warms her heart whenever he chooses to share it. However, the truth is he's as gorgeous as Asher and could easily be a model himself, or a professional actor.

Of course, he says the same thing about her, but she gazes into the mirror often enough to know the truth. She's as ordinary as they come, character actor material, at best, if acting was her goal (which it isn't). Not being awash in vanity like Kristen or Olivia, and having little interest in clothes or other teen-centric superficialities like makeup or fancy hairstyles, she and Donovan complement one another perfectly, even to the point of hating how they look on camera, all of which has fused their friendship over the years into an unbreakable bond.

Mr. Ketchum steps over to them. "Now, I know I'll see you here tomorrow for the school scenes, but you also have my cell number in case any complications arise throughout the week."

Cassie nods. "No worries, Mr. K. D-Boy and me have it all covered."

"D-Boy?" Donovan raises quizzical eyebrows. "When did you come up with that one?"

"Just now." She grins. "Like it?"

He shrugs. "It could grow on me."

Mr. Ketchum laughs. "Go on, you two. I'll see you tomorrow at noon."

They laugh and Cassie leads the way to the door, turning as Mrs. Ketchum stands and offers a smile. "Thanks for training such good actors, Mrs. K."

"That's my job, Cassie. Enjoy your week off."

As they cross the campus toward the student parking lot, dodging excited teens itching to start their spring break, Cassie feels penetrating eyes fixed on her back. Maybe it's a lifetime of watching horror flicks, but her sensitivity to being surreptitiously watched has always been ultra-high. As is Donovan's ultra-sensitivity to her moods.

"What's up, Cass?"

She stops and he halts beside her. "I'm being watched. Or we are." She spins like a pirouetting dancer and spots a black hoodie duck behind the large shade tree in the center of the quad. "It's Jaden again."

Donovan squints against the bright afternoon sun. "I don't see him."

"Behind the shade tree. Come on, let's go."

She grabs his arm and turns him around, leading him back toward the parking lot. As they walk, she marvels as always at her amazing school, how it looks like something out of a sci-fi film. They stroll past the Performing Arts Center; having no windows, it resembles a massive upside-down golden funnel that leans to one side and sports a flat roof. She loves watching plays in the Center because the acoustics are perfect, whether you sit in the orchestra section or up in the nosebleed balconies.

"I've noticed him watching us a lot lately, especially on set," he remarks, but he doesn't sound as creeped out as Cassie feels. "I figured maybe it was because he was waiting for us to need him for some job or other. He's so dedicated."

"He's been watching us at school too," she says, keeping her voice neutral as they brush past chattering groups of students near the Dance Building, which looks like a Star Destroyer from *Star Wars* crashed into the ground with the "engine" portion bending back at an angle toward the sky.

"Maybe he has a crush on you," he adds, giving her a friendly nudge.

"I've considered that, but it doesn't seem likely."

"Why not? You're stupendously awesome."

She considers a moment. "I don't notice him watching unless I'm with you."

"He's probably jealous of me like every other guy who's into you. They all think we're gonna get together, even though we keep saying we're not."

"Yeah, that's possible."

He pauses a moment, eyeing her uncertainly. "We aren't, are we?"

She studies his tentative demeanor, seeing in him what she always sees—the only boy she can ever imagine dating, even though they never have, at least not in any romantic sense. They've talked about it in a round-about sort of way, but never decided on anything.

She grins. "Not at the moment."

He returns the grin as they pass through an open gate into the student parking lot, where they skirt milling students and moving cars until they arrive at Cassie's powder blue Civic.

Donovan tosses both of their backpacks into the rear seat and plops into the passenger side while she slides behind the wheel. Somehow the car's interior always smells new after it's been sitting in the sun, and the pleasant aroma makes Cassie smile as she slips on her seat belt. She likes the car and the boy sitting beside her. The smile remains as she eases out of the parking lot.

They swing by Donovan's white, two-story house to drop off his school stuff and grab the shooting schedule and storyboards—shot by shot drawings of the entire film, drawn by Donovan—and to remind his mom that he'll be at Cassie's for dinner. Dinner at Cassie's is a regular "thing" for them because Donovan's mom works a lot of nightshifts, and if she doesn't have time to prepare food ahead of time, he usually just microwaves frozen dinners.

Short and stout and dressed in her Caribbean blue nurse's uniform, name badge firmly affixed to the upper left side, with dark hair tied back off her face, Marjory Quinn greets them as they enter. "Hi Hun. How was school today?"

"Great," Donovan replies, grinning. "Everyone loved our footage."

Her brown eyes cloud over with distaste and she frowns, but then shifts to a partial smile. "Yes, the horror stuff. Hopefully, you'll outgrow it one day."

Donovan sighs and Cassie touches his arm as a gesture of comfort.

"Mom, I'm eighteen and you know I plan to make horror films my career. You'll just have to deal."

"You'll change your mind," she says in that condescending tone Cassie hates. "Children always do."

Donovan glances at Cassie and shrugs. This is standard procedure for his mom, which is another reason he spends so much of his time at her house.

Marjory scoops car keys out of a colorful wicker basket sitting atop a small round table near the door. "I won't be home till morning and I know it's Friday, but don't stay late at your girlfriend's house again."

Cassie and Donovan exchange another glance of consternation. "She's my best friend, mom, not my girlfriend."

She smiles knowingly. "Your late father was my best friend until he became my boyfriend. It'll happen."

She turns her cheek, and he dutifully leans in to kiss it.

"Don't work too hard, Mom."

"How can I not? It's a hospital." She swooshes past him out the front door.

Cassie and Donovan lock eyes for a long moment before shaking their heads and heading upstairs to his room.

Cassie loves the retro feel to Donovan's room. Just like his clothes, he loves collecting old pieces of furniture, bedding, lamps, and other stuff from thrift stores. He's especially fond of 80s items and often buys them off eBay if he finds a good deal. He has a huge vinyl collection, while everyone else she knows listens to digital music on their phones. Even CDs are pretty much out these days. But Donovan keeps the needle on his turntable in perfect condition and she enjoys listening to his oldies.

He's even got a tube television that still works. It's in color, but the picture quality is nothing like her flat screen at home. His bedcover is a muted pink and his pillowcases are purple and red. His walls are adorned with horror movie posters (what else?)—all films they've watched together, including his all-time favorite, the original black and white Universal classic, *The Wolfman*.

Her current favorite is the 2018 *Halloween* because Jamie Lee Curtis portrayed such a kick-ass woman who determined she would not be victimized ever again. That poster adorns *her* bedroom wall.

He tosses his backpack on the desk chair and rummages around on his neatly-arranged desktop for the storyboards and shot sheets. He likes writing everything down, while she stores notes, locations, shot and call sheets in her tablet. Both of them, however, have contact info for cast and crew in their phones, just in case.

He spins a few ABBA tunes on the turntable, and they sprawl out on the bed side by side to listen. Cassie enjoys ABBA's chirpy, catchy style, which is different from other Pop music she's heard. She's bursting with excitement about the week to come, but senses Donovan needs a few minutes of downtime, maybe because of the "mom" thing. She's a nice lady overall, but has always wanted him to be someone he's not. She doesn't push super hard, but like the incident downstairs, she implies that he's still a child and will outgrow everything he likes. It hurts him deeply, so Cassie does her best to be supportive.

Without warning, he sits up and hops off the bed.

"We better go."

Edward Stewart is laying out ingredients for dinner when Cassie and Donovan stroll into the kitchen. "How's my favorite scream team?"

Cassie smiles as he engulfs her in a hug, reaching out a long arm to pull in Donovan, as well.

"Okay, daddy, you're crushing us, as usual."

She laughs and he releases them.

Donovan tosses her dad a lopsided grin and doesn't look the least bit embarrassed. "Hi, Pop."

Edward winks and turns back to the kitchen counter, which is laid out with veggies, chicken strips, and large tortillas.

Cassie loves how her dad treats Donovan like a son, and Donovan truly thinks of him as his dad. Never having known his own father, and with Edward always having wanted a son, it's worked out perfectly for them both.

Cassie's mouth begins to water. Her dad makes the most amazing chicken burritos she's ever eaten. For such a big man, he's almost delicate when he manipulates utensils and sprinkles ingredients into his dishes. She's often encouraged him to go on one of those cooking shows because his talents are so amazing, but he refuses.

"So, how did everyone like your footage?"

Wearing the bright red apron sporting "Kitchen Elf" in green letters that she gave him last Christmas, Edward looks like a cartoon character, especially with his wide shoulders and old-school flat-top buzz-cut tinged with gray around the temples. He chops the chicken and veggies so hard and fast that the rapid *thunk thunk thunk* against the cutting board sounds like muted machine gun fire.

Cassie and Donovan slip onto barstools, which line the counter that serves as one side of their kitchen. The stove rests dead center and the sink sits beneath double windows looking out into the decent-sized backyard. Cassie typically eats breakfast in here—because there's also a dinette set—and dinner too if her dad has to work nights and doesn't have time to cook beforehand.

"They loved it," she announces proudly.

"Not a single dig on our footage," Donovan adds, looking relaxed, elbows propped back on the countertop. "I think we have a winner."

"You think?" Cassie tosses him a chastising look. "We wrote and directed it, so of course it's fantastic."

He chuckles. "Now you sound like Kristen."

She snatches a potholder off a metal rack behind her and chucks it at him. "That's a low blow."

He ducks to one side, dislodging the fedora, and the potholder strikes her dad in the back. He tosses them a look of mock annoyance.

"Hey, time-out back there. You kill the cook, you don't eat." He grins and returns to his chopping. "I'm glad it went well. You still planning to enter it in that competition?"

"Of course," Cassie and Donovan spit out simultaneously as he replaces the fedora onto his mop of hair.

Hat securely in place, Donovan hops off his stool. "Let us give you a hand, Pop."

Normally, Cassie's dad begs off their help, but this time he asks them to heat up the tortilla warmer—a round machine resembling a waffle iron that's strictly for tortillas—and to warm up the black beans on the stove.

As always, dinner is a relaxed affair as Cassie and Donovan regale Edward with the goings on at school. Being a performing arts high school in Southern California, it seems to Cassie that the kids are even more dramatic than those at regular schools, being performers on the cusp of Hollywood, and all. Every little thing becomes a major "I'm ready for my close up" moment.

"Just today, Dad, this girl in the cafeteria acted like she would die because she got cheddar cheese on her burger instead of Swiss."

Donovan nearly spits out his water. "Oh, my God, that was funny. She deserves an Oscar, seriously. Best performance by an entitled brat."

Edward laughs and takes a bite of his burrito. The salsa dribbles down his chin and onto his plate. Cassie laughs and hands him a napkin.

He wipes away the dripping salsa. "So, everything set for filming?"

They nod simultaneously.

"My buddy over at Star Security will have the key for the warehouse. Just text him the day before to remind him. I gave you his number, right?"

Cassie nods. "Yep. Bob Washington. I've got it."

"We're so stoked you snagged that set for us," Donovan blurts, barely containing his excitement. "That creepy warehouse is perfect for our finale."

Edward grins. "Just make sure to give me a credit at the end—'creepy warehouse location snagged by Edward Stewart.'" He swigs from his glass of beer.

"You got it," Donovan exclaims, holding up his hand for a high five.

Edward slaps it.

The *Theme from SWAT* blasts through the room like a blizzard, startling the kids. Edward looks sheepish as he pulls the phone from his pocket.

"Sorry, I forgot to put it on vibrate." He glances at the number and frowns. "It's the sergeant. Sorry, I have to take this." He stands and steps away from the table. "Yeah, Sergeant, what's up?"

Cassie and Donovan exchange a look. Using electronic devices at the table is forbidden in the Stewart home, but then, the sergeant doesn't usually call Edward at home. They watch as he listens, phone pressed to his ear, standing a few feet from the table in front of a painting of an enormous wave breaking against a pristine beach. Cassie loves that painting. Her mom completed it shortly before she died.

Edward ends his call and absently slides the phone back into his front pants pocket.

When he looks troubled, but doesn't speak, Cassie says, "Dad? Everything okay?"

"I have to work after all."

"You promised we'd hang out tonight, the three of us." Cassie can't hide her disappointment. He's been working too many nightshifts lately and she misses having him around.

Edward nods, his expression grave. "That was before somebody decided to take Friday the Thirteenth too far."

"What do you mean?" Donovan asks, his smooth brows knitted with confusion.

"Somebody was spotted in one of those hockey masks and overalls leaving Pierson Park just after dark."

Cassie shrugs. "So? I'm sure lots of fans dress up like that every Friday the Thirteenth."

Edward nods. "But most of 'em don't commit murder."

"What?" Shocked, she glances at Donovan, whose olive skin pales.

"Sergeant didn't give me all the details, but the killing was pretty brutal, like in one of those Jason movies you guys watch. He wants every officer out on patrol tonight, cruising the parks and keeping a lookout for weird stuff going down."

Cassie locks eyes with Donovan. "We just filmed there last weekend."

"Which is why I'm happy you're not filming tonight because it would've been canceled," Edward asserts, his no-arguments tone in full timbre. "You keep the doors and windows locked."

"What about taking Donovan home?"

He shakes his head. "I don't want either of you out tonight. Donovan can crash on my bed. I won't be back till morning anyway." He glances at Donovan. "That work for you, pal?"

Looking rattled by the development, Donovan nods. "Uh, yeah, sure. Thanks."

"I need to suit up and get down to the station." Edward hurries from the dining room and Cassie hears the door to his bedroom close with a *click*.

A heavy silence settles over the dining room, and despite the pleasant odor of freshly cooked food, it chills her to the bone.

"That's so weird, a Jason murder right after we..." Cassie lets the thought trail off.

Donovan, as always, is on the same wavelength. "Filmed a murder inspired by *Friday the 13th* in that same park."

She nods, brushing some reddish curls away from her eyes. "Except we didn't film the kill scene at the park. We used your backyard."

"Yeah, but it's supposed to take place in that park."

"I wonder if my dad'll find out exactly how the person was killed."

"Are you thinking it could be the same? That's not possible."

She considers a moment. "Ordinarily, no. But what if…?

"What?"

"What if someone was spying on us when we filmed that scene and then decided to act it out for real?"

That's…" He meets her wide-eyed gaze. "Scary as hell."

CHAPTER TWO

CASSIE TAKES CHARGE

Cassie's sleep is troubled. She tosses and turns as visions of Jason stalking her film crew torment her overactive brain. He lurks behind every tree and swings his machete at them with wild abandon. Knowing that Donovan is just down the hall brings her a smidgen of comfort, but the troubling feeling that their set locations are being spied upon refuses to even consider going away.

Exhausted and unable to feel even a bit rested, she throws off her twisted bedcovers at seven the next morning, despite it being the first day of spring break. With a noon call time at school, she decides a cup of coffee might taste good, so she trudges down the long hall in her pajamas to the kitchen.

She should be surprised to find Donovan seated at the counter hugging a steaming mug of hot chocolate and staring into space, but she isn't. They are too much alike to be surprised by anything anymore. His distaste for coffee is a rare area of disagreement.

He looks up and offers that shy little smile that always makes her heart flutter, but her eyes bulge in amazement at his extreme case of bedhead. He looks like he stuck his finger into the proverbial light socket. Brown hair juts out in all directions and, coupled with his bright red pajamas and blood-spattered *Walking Dead* bathrobe, he looks like an escapee from the loony bin.

"I know what you're thinking," he says, smirking as he sips his chocolate. "But seriously, the Bride of Frankenstein has nothing on you."

Her mouth drops open in shock as the image of Elsa Lanchester with her conical hairdo and white lightning-trace streaks on each side invades her weary brain. "I didn't even check my own bedhead. That bad, huh?"

He sips and nods. "You didn't sleep well either?"

She shakes her head. "I'm going to be paranoid someone's watching us today."

"Well, the whole crew will be watching us, but I know what you mean. Any message from your dad?"

She unplugs her phone from the kitchen outlet and opens the message app. "No."

She sets down her phone and turns to start the coffee maker, but it's already percolating. She's surprised she didn't notice the aroma before.

I must be really tired.

"Thanks for putting on the coffee."

"No prob."

She slides onto a barstool beside him as she waits for the coffee maker to beep.

"Do you think we'll have any drama from Mr. Warner today?"

He shrugs. "He's Mr. K's old friend, right?"

"More like an acquaintance who washed his Hollywood career down the drain, to quote Mr. K."

"I know he's supposed to be 'temperamental'"—Donovan uses air quotes—"and a lecher, but I'm sure Mr. K talked to him about not giving us kids a hard time or hitting on any of the girls."

"I'm sure he did, but you know actors. They don't listen."

"Like Kristen. And Robert." Donovan's face clouds over with uncharacteristic anger. "Are you sure you're cool having that jerk around?"

She shrugs. "I can handle him. Besides, we kill him off tonight and then he's done."

"I'm looking forward to that scene." He sips his hot chocolate. "Too bad I can't be the actor who kills him."

The coffee maker beeps, and Cassie smiles as she pads across the kitchen to pour herself a cup.

By the time she showers and brushes out her thick, auburn curls, slips on loose jeans and a long-sleeved pullover shirt, and heads back downstairs, Donovan has already cleaned up and shoved his mop of hair beneath a red felt fedora. The mismatched pastel colors of his shirt and corduroy pants only add to his addled, starving artist look.

"Dad."

She's surprised to see her father sitting at the kitchen table nursing a mug of coffee. He wears his police blues and looks exhausted. No, more than exhausted. His slumped posture and sagging shoulders make him look… disheartened. Donovan is sitting across from him, wearing a look of morbid trepidation on his face.

"Morning, Cass." Her dad offers a weak smile and nods toward the empty chair beside him.

Feeling the somber mood pressing in on her, she eases into the chair. "So, was the killer caught?"

He shakes his head, slurping noisily from his coffee. Cassie notes the thick steam rising from the mug, amazed that he doesn't burn his throat.

"No, and everything was quiet on my route."

Cassie exchanges a worried look with Donovan. "There's something you're both not telling me."

Donovan doesn't answer, so she turns back to her father.

He gives her a sober look. "Seems like the perp used some kind of arrow, or maybe the spear from a spear gun to puncture the victim's throat. From underneath a park bench while the guy slept."

Cassie stiffens, her heartrate accelerating.

"Could be a coincidence, but that sounds pretty close to your movie, right?"

She nods. "What do you think it means, Dad?"

"I don't know. It's not my area. Homicide is investigating."

"Do they know about our movie?" Donovan's boyish voice sounds shaky.

"Not yet, but I'll have to tell them. Right now, they figure the perp got the idea from the first Jason movie, and that's probably true. In the meantime, I want you to be extra careful. Never let anyone wander off alone from your set, even in broad daylight."

They both nod.

"Where are you filming tonight?"

"Baxter's house," they answer simultaneously.

Donovan indicates that Cassie should continue.

"We have another kill scene tonight, in front of the house."

Edward sits back and considers a long moment, the laugh lines around his eyes creased with worry.

Spooked as she is, Cassie desperately hopes her dad won't insist she cancel the night shoots. A horror film without night scenes might as well be a Disney princess movie.

"I'm on patrol again tonight," Edward finally says, fixing his intense gaze on her like she's being interrogated. "I'll make sure to swing by your location at regular intervals. If you see anything suspicious, or anyone hanging around who shouldn't be there, text me at once."

"We will," Cassie assures him, glancing at Donovan, who nods vigorously.

Edward looks satisfied. "I'm going to crash now. Break a leg today, or whatever they say to filmmakers."

Cassie cracks a smile. "That's for actors, but it'll work. Thanks, Dad."

He offers a lopsided grin and rises from the table. Scooping up his peaked cap, he slogs his way out of the kitchen.

Cassie and Donovan sit in silence, listening to his footfalls on the creaky wooden floor as he enters his bedroom.

Donovan tries for a reassuring look. "It's probably like he said, some nut copying *Friday the 13th*."

She nods, but isn't convinced. "Probably. Come on, let's go over our set ups and shot sheets. I want everything to go smoothly."

"Me too."

Performing Arts Academy High School looks lonesome with the students gone, like one of those apocalyptic zombie movies where everyone's vanished or died. Jaden, clad in his black hoodie, despite the warm temperature, stands beside a tee-shirt-clad Mr. K when Cassie pulls her dad's SUV into the parking lot and the two of them help her and Donovan unload the equipment.

Most of the day's shooting will take place inside the Film Building - a half triangle with a box on top that juts sharply into the sky. They'll lens the exterior scenes in the adjacent quad area. All the equipment is placed around a picnic table not far from the shade tree, convenient to all filming sites. As Cassie sets her tablet onto the metal table, she realizes how much she'll miss this home-away-from-home after she graduates in June.

Unlike most high schools, there are no sports fields or even a gym, because there are no sports. Being a performing arts school, besides having the performance hall for live shows, there's also a large screening room to watch student-made films, numerous dance studios, and a lot of acting spaces. All the kids get their state mandated PE credit through dance and movement classes. The money PAAHS saves by not having sports teams has gone into top-of-the-line facilities, cameras, sound systems, speakers, microphones, and lights. This school is for kids who are dead serious about a career in the arts, which, for Cassie, is what makes the place so much fun.

The cast and crew arrive promptly at their appointed times, which excites Cassie because their punctuality demonstrates a serious commitment to the film.

While she and William review shot-sheets at the table under the shade tree, she can't help noticing Olivia over near the cafeteria, which is shaped like the hull of the starship Enterprise. Cassie is close enough to overhear Olivia boldly flirting with Diego, Robert, and Asher at the same time.

Robert wears another tight tank top that efficiently displays his arms and six-pack, while Diego and Asher wear their "character" clothes—Asher sloppy style and Diego grunge.

Olivia squeezes Diego's bicep with one hand and Robert's with the other. "I don't know which one is harder. Any idea who's stronger?"

Diego looks embarrassed while Robert smirks. "That would be me, right, Diego? I'm the only athlete at this school." He tosses off a double bicep flex and Oliva giggles.

Cassie shakes her head in disgust.

"Whatever," Diego says to Robert, looking at Asher as though hoping the other boy will save him. "We all know you hit the weights, Robert, but Asher's a skater. That's pretty athletic."

"Hey, don't get me into this macho man-off," Asher retorts scornfully. "I'm not into that stuff."

Olivia sidles closer to him, giving him the once over, like she's never paid much attention before.

"You don't have to be with those gorgeous eyes and beautiful curly hair." She runs her hand though his moppy 'fro and rubs up against him.

He's clearly annoyed by her obsequious manner. "I'm gonna shadow William, since I'm basically playing him in the movie." He eyes Diego and Robert. "Have fun, guys."

He wanders off to join Cassie and William, who welcome him into their discussion.

Robert looks annoyed that Olivia has now focused entirely on Diego, but then he spots a group of arriving girls—all of whom play student extras—heading in his direction. Without a backward glance at Olivia, he charges forward into their midst, grinning and preening.

"Welcome, ladies," he announces like he's the MC of a game show, and then follows them toward some empty benches near the Film Building, just past Mr. K's open classroom door.

Cassie feels sorry for those girls because Robert is nothing but a flirt, and they apparently don't see it because they look flattered by his empty compliments. She glances back at Olivia, who's laughing flirtatiously at something Diego apparently said, and hopes Kristen doesn't notice. That's the last thing they need now—a real-life catfight.

In front of the Performing Arts Building, Mrs. Ketchum sits before a foldable table laid out with makeup supplies and a large mirror. She's touching up Kristen's makeup.

"I'm so excited to film a scene with you, Mrs. K."

Mrs. K, looking very business-like in a staid pantsuit and low-heeled shoes, smiles graciously.

"You flatter me too much, Kristen. My role as Principal Loomis is a mere cameo. However, I do think it's amusing that my character is named after Dr. Loomis in the Halloween movies. Donald Pleasance always seemed like such a cordial man."

Kristen stares at Mrs. K's reflection in the mirror, her deep blue eyes brimming with hero worship.

"If Cassie and Donovan manage to get this film into a few decent festivals, you'll be remembered as a great actress and maybe get some *real* work. You told me before you missed Hollywood."

The older woman's face clouds over. "I've attempted a comeback several times, but unlike men with bad-boy reputations, the business isn't as forgiving of women, especially women of vintage."

"That's so unfair!"

"It's a young woman's profession, Kristen, which is why you'll excel."

She finishes touching up Kristen's subtle makeup, making her look like the sweet, unassuming high school girl she's playing.

Mrs. K nods approvingly. "You look beautiful."

Kristen grins. "And you look like a star."

Ron Warner, the actor playing the teacher, has a later call time because Mr. K feels "the less he's on set, the better."

That makes Donovan wonder, so he asks, "Why did you recommend him if he's such a pain?"

Mr. K, dressed in a tee shirt and wrinkled slacks, shrugs as he clamps a light into place on its metal stand and secures it with a twist. "It was actually Asher who suggested him."

"Asher?" That catches Donovan by surprise. "How does Asher even know who the guy is?"

As Donovan reaches for another stand, Mr. K grabs the key light and prepares to affix it to the clamp.

"Asher says he watches old movies with his mom, and she likes Warner. He remembered that I knew Warner and made the suggestion."

Sounds reasonable, Donovan thinks as he holds the stand steady so Mr. K can fasten the key light and lock it into place. The key light is the primary one used to illuminate a scene, so its positioning is critical. As Director of Photography, William will place it correctly when he sets up the camera.

"But you didn't answer my first question, Mr. K. If Warner is a such pain to work with, why have him around?"

Mr. K tosses off a smile. "Well, he won't cost you any money, for one thing. He also has a name, sort of, that might help you at festivals, and he's a good actor. The fact that he used to be a lecherous drunk might not be an issue anymore. People *can* change, Donovan."

Filming has been progressing well for the past hour and Cassie is happy they're on schedule. All the high school scenes need to be shot today and that means forty different camera setups, which is a huge number for a single day. Fortunately, the exteriors use mostly natural lighting and William often uses a Steadicam, which eliminates the need to constantly move and reset the tripod because all he has to do is walk around and follow the action. Thankfully, the school bought a first-rate Steadicam (a camera carrier that's strapped to the cameraman so he can move it around freely) for the film program, and it's a lifesaver, as far as Cassie is concerned.

Trouble begins the moment Mr. Warner shows up to film his teacher scenes. As Mr. K told her and Donovan during the planning stage, Warner's an actor of some fame, mostly on old daytime soap operas and TV movies. For a middle-aged guy, he's still big and solid, having clearly stayed in shape, and has rugged good looks that Cassie admits might help the film. However, since most viewers of horror movies are boys and men, Warner's appearance probably won't matter too much.

His name *might* draw in fanboys of his one and only horror film, *The House of Horror*, a cheesy direct-to-DVD potboiler about a haunted house that eats its residents. While it's true that Warner pickled his career along with himself in alcohol-fueled binges and then buried what remained under a barrage of sexual harassment charges, moviegoers love seeing washed up actors make a comeback.

The problem, Cassie soon realizes, is that Warner hasn't learned from his past mistakes.

Inside the classroom, she's huddled with William going over the scene while Donovan preps the actors. This single-take sequence involves Kristen and Olivia, who (amazingly) play best friends in the film, passing notes back and forth about the character played by Diego. The teacher, named Mr. Talbot (chosen by Donovan as a tribute to the tortured main character in *The Wolfman*) and played by Warner, is supposed to intercept one of the notes and chastise them for wasting their time chasing a boy when they should be focused on filmmaking, not to mention the real killer at large in their community.

Once William has marked with painter's tape the spots where he'll stop while roaming with the Steadicam, Cassie glances around for Mr. and Mrs. Ketchum, but doesn't spot them. She knows Mr. K doesn't like to make his student directors feel uncomfortable by watching while they direct, and Mrs. K's cameo isn't for a while yet. She motions to Donovan, who breaks away from Asher to hurry over.

"They ready to shoot it?"

"Yeah, but I don't know where Warner wandered off to. Again." He chews his lower lip, looking distressed.

Cassie hears a howl of protest from Kristen and a few choice words that would easily get the film rated R if she included them. She turns to see Kristen and Olivia, more enraged than your average werewolf, storming up the aisle toward her and Donovan as though to rip their throats out.

Warner, wearing a blue button-down shirt and black slacks, leans insolently against the classroom doorjamb. He tosses off a "what did I do?" look and leers at Cassie.

Kristen—her face a tornado of rage—plants herself before Cassie and Donovan and points at the smirking Warner.

"You two better do something with that creep, or I'm going to kick him in the balls so hard he'll squeal like a pig!"

"It's bad enough that he's been leering at us all day," Olivia continues, like they have the script prewritten, "but now he keeps getting in my space and rubbing up against me. Not cool at all!"

Cassie eyes Donovan uncertainly, and then both of them study Warner, still leaning against the doorjamb and smirking. Momentarily flummoxed about what course of action she should take, Cassie spots the phone in Donovan's hand and a brilliant idea hits her like a club.

"I'll handle this," she assures the girls, grabbing Donovan's phone and striding purposefully between the rows of desks to stop right in front of Warner.

Despite feeling insecure standing up to an adult in this way, she calls on all the acting lessons she ever received to be convincing.

"Mr. Warner, Mr. K told me you're hoping this film might restore your credibility in Hollywood, that acting responsibly on a student film might convince producers to take another chance on you."

Warner loses the smirk and looks confused, like he'd expected her to yell at him. "Why, yes, my dear, that is my hope."

She offers a sweet smile. "I prefer Cassie or Director, thank you very much. As I was saying, you're in a film made by teenagers and every one of them has a phone. They've been filming you all morning and will continue to do so for the rest of the shoot, especially when I tell them to."

His look of confusion deepens the makeup-covered wrinkles on his face and he glances around at the crew members. A glowering Asher films the exchange.

"I'm afraid I don't understand, my—Cassie."

She leans in conspiratorially, hoping she sounds convincing. "Well, see, it's like this. Teens like me love to post stuff on social media, and vids of you harassing teenage girls will go viral for sure, especially with the hashtag 'me too' attached. I bet those Hollywood producers will *love* watching them, don't you?"

He pales beneath the makeup and, suddenly devoid of cockiness, runs a nervous hand through his slicked-back, thinning dark hair as he glances again at the cast and crew. This time they're all holding their phones, filming the exchange.

Cassie wants to hug every one of them for catching on so quickly, especially Asher, who practically growls at Warner like an angry tiger ready to pounce. But she keeps her composure and offers the older man another sugary smile.

"Just think, Mr. Warner, you'll finally become an internet star."

Heart pounding like a bass drum, she turns and saunters back up the aisle toward Donovan and the girls, forcing herself to appear cool and collected, even though she's anything but.

Donovan grins like there's no tomorrow, but Kristen and Olivia look stunned, like they can't believe she's done what she's just done. Honestly, she can't believe it either and wishes her dad had been there to see her in action.

Donovan leans in to her ear. "That was stellar."

"Thanks." She hands him back his phone and turns to the girls. "I don't think he'll bother you anymore today."

For once, Kristen offers a genuine smile and even Olivia grins with delight. Then they realize how close they're standing to each other and dart away down the aisles like repelling magnets.

"Now let's shoot this scene, shall we?" Cassie waves at the student actors to sit at their desks as the tension in her body drains away now that the confrontation is over.

Warner takes his place beside the teacher's desk, giving her a wide berth as he passes, like she might slap him.

Mr. K stands just inside the doorway and catches Cassie's eye from across the room, mouthing, "Well played."

She grins, suddenly feeling rock solid inside, like she just passed a major test on her road to Hollywood. Once all the student actors are in their seats, the now very compliant and professional Mr. Warner assumes his proper role as their teacher, all business.

While Cassie directs the scene and watches the monitor, Donovan watches the live actors. Both are looking for any issues that may need to be fixed in subsequent takes. They alternate these roles each day so that they share equally in the directorial duties.

As the dialogue moves beyond the passing of notes and on to the recent murders that seem to be patterned after a film the class is shooting, Cassie's mind wanders to what her dad said about the killer of the previous night. What if the murderer *is* copying the script she and Donovan wrote, just like the fictional killer in the film within the film? How would the killer know that script unless he's somehow spying on the production? Or worse, what if—?

"Cassie, cut," Donovan hisses from behind her. "Scene's over."

Snapping out of her dark thoughts, Cassie calls "Cut," and turns to Donovan, feeling the color of embarrassment rise to her cheeks. "Sorry. How'd it look to you?"

"It looked fine from my end, but how'd it look on the monitor? Did William get everything?"

Cassie realizes she spaced out halfway through the scene, a major no-no for a director. Attempting to recover her aplomb, she announces to the room at large, "Good work everyone, especially you, William. Let's do it again for safety."

And this time I won't let my mind wander, but she doesn't say that.

She waits for Mr. Warner to resume his place at the front of the class and then signals William.

"Camera rolling," he says, pointing the video camera at Warner and pauses a moment for the camera to begin recording. "Speed."

"Action," Cassie says, and the scene replays. This time she scrutinizes all the action on the monitor while William skillfully moves his camera among the various students, who express their fear over who the killer could be and when he might strike again.

The scene plays out without a hitch and Cassie forgets about the real murder in her excitement over this lengthy, perfectly executed, sequence. Single-take scenes involving a group of actors are always risky because if someone flubs even one line, the entire scene must be reshot because there is nothing to cut away to.

"Perfect, guys," she proclaims excitedly. "Thanks so much, everyone, for being so prepared. Actors, take five while we set up for the next scene."

She notices Donovan eyeing her with concern, but tosses off her cocky smile to reassure him. It works. He tips his hat and sets about having the crew rearrange the classroom for a sequence that takes place on a different day.

It's dusk by the time all the interior and exterior school scenes are shot, so the actors who are not needed for the night shoot are sent home. As Cassie stands beneath a gorgeous red and gold California sunset watching them exit through the main gate, her mind returns to her earlier fears about who might have killed that man in the park.

Could it possibly be one of these kids she's known for the past four years? Her dad has often told her stories of people he thought he knew turning to crime because something traumatic changed them. Could that have happened to one of her classmates? The thought is too terrifying to entertain, so she pushes it to the back of her mind. With her dad's stern admonition to not let anyone wander off the set ringing loudly in her ears, she keeps a close eye on all her actors until they've vanished into the twilight.

Next up is Baxter's house. Tonight's kill is patterned after the iconic scene in the original *Halloween* when The Shape used a kitchen knife to pin Annie's boyfriend to the wall. That's the "hook" of their script—the student film within the film is replicating kill scenes from some of the most famous horror films ever made.

A light breeze rustles her frizzy hair, and she warmly recalls her and Donovan having so much fun watching those classic films to decide which ones to pay homage to in their script.

Lost in thought, she turns to re-enter the school and nearly collides with Robert, stifling a startled cry of surprise. He blocks the path, his facial expression disturbing. It's part leer and part excitement, the setting sun silhouetting his tall, muscular frame into something almost monstrous.

Forcing calm into her voice, she says, "Why are you out here, Robert? You should be rehearsing with Donovan."

He takes a menacing step closer. "It won't be true dark for a while yet. Plenty of downtime for you and me to hang out."

Cassie's heart pounds and her temper rises. "We've done this before, Robert. I'm not into you and never will be."

The leer increases, like he's a charismatic serial killer sizing up his next victim. "You can't know that till you kiss me."

Faster than Cassie would have thought possible, he lunges forward and plants his lips on hers. She's startled, but her dad's self-defense training kicks in and she thrusts her knee hard into his groin before his thick veiny arms can get halfway around her back.

Robert grunts and his face collapses in agony as he crumples to the concrete walkway, grabbing his privates and writhing about like he's on fire. "Shit, Cass!"

Cassie trembles with rage. She hadn't even realized her level of anger as she swipes a hand across her lips and has to fight the urge to kick him again.

"I knew I'd regret letting you be in this film. You're fired, Robert."

Still unable to stand, he gapes up at her in shock. "You can't fire me. I'm tonight's victim."

She's tempted to say something super snarky about how she would love to be the one who kills him, but fights to regain control. As a director, she can't let actors, or anyone else, get to her.

"You're an expendable extra, Robert, and I just expended you. We'll find an actor who keeps his hands to himself."

His face contorts with animalistic rage. "No one treats me like this! I'll get payback. You hear me, Cassie?"

She stalks back into the school, ignoring his continued invectives, but shivering at the hatred behind them.

Maybe she never really knew Robert after all.

CHAPTER THREE

THE SECOND MURDER

"H E WHAT?" DONOVAN'S FACE TURNS thundery when Cassie recounts the Robert incident, his fists clenching and unclenching in a way she's never seen from him.

She places a hand on his arm, feeling the tightness of his muscles. "It's okay, Donovan, you know I can take care of myself. I kneed him where it counts and then fired him."

His venomous threats echo in her mind, but she makes sure not to tell Donovan about them. He might confront Robert and get seriously hurt.

Donovan's perfect eyebrows fly upward in surprise and his arm beneath her hand relaxes. He takes in a deep breath and releases it before pulling a grin, his teeth almost glowing in the gathering gloom.

"Good call on both counts." Then the smile slips from his face like a mask and he unclenches his fists. "Except now there's no student victim tonight."

"I thought about that walking back here and I have the perfect solution."

"What?"

She presses a gentle finger into his chest. "You."

He stiffens again, glancing down so the fedora shadows his hazel eyes. "You know I'm not thrilled with acting."

She offers an encouraging smile. "You may not be thrilled with it, but you're really good at it. Much better than me. If a director of this film should have a cameo, it *has* to be you."

He looks up and meets her gaze in the deepening dusk, but remains silent.

"Please? For me?" She offers a sly smile. "We put Diego and Asher in the movie, so it's only right the third cutest boy at this school should have a part."

His beautiful eyes widen in shocked surprise at her flattery which, quite frankly, surprises her too. Where did that comment come from? She usually plays it close to the vest with compliments, probably because everyone is so paranoid these days about saying something that might be considered harassment. Sure, if he'd said that to her and she didn't like it, she could holler "harassment" and get attention, but it doesn't usually work in reverse. Maybe it should.

The smile creeping across his shadowed features indicates he's not offended, which relieves her mind and, for other reasons, causes her heart to flutter with unaccustomed edginess.

"The third cutest, huh?"

Biting her lip, she grins and nods.

"Okay."

She gives him a quick hug. "Thanks, D-Boy."

Feeling oddly self-conscious, she pulls back before he can return the hug.

He doesn't seem to mind, his face now completely hidden in shadow. The red and gold sky has settled into a low burnt orange and the sun is no longer visible over the top of the Performing Arts Center.

"Do me one favor," he says just as she's turning toward the crew members hauling equipment out of the quad.

She turns back, searching for his face in the dark. She can't see it, but she knows he's smiling by the amused tone of his voice.

"Next time you kick Robert in the balls, have someone film it so I can watch."

She laughs and grabs his arm. "C'mon, let's shut down this set."

Cassie has gathered alongside Donovan, Kristen, Diego, Asher, and Jaden on Baxter's expansive front lawn, close to the sidewalk. Crew members mill around the front of the two-story Cape Cod-style home, which is painted white with blue trim and sports three gables showcasing drapery-covered second-floor windows. Lights glow weakly behind those drapes, and a single porch light reflects off the shiny, red-lacquered front door.

Studio lights on tripods have been set into position while William, dressed in his usual cargo shorts and wrinkled, metal-band tee, aims the camera at the corner of the house where a stone path leads into the back-yard.

Baxter, clad in a shirt two sizes too big and striped Bermuda shorts, uses a remote control to operate his drone, hovering it above the house and the surrounding residential streets. In the thick darkness above the street-lights, the drone resembles a large, many-legged insect buzzing overhead as though preparing to swoop in and attack. Baxter operates the controls with his right hand while snagging tortilla chip after tortilla chip from a fanny pack and shoving them into his mouth with his left.

Cassie's entire body is twisted into knots because this is a kill scene and, in the back of her mind, she fears that the real killer might be spying on them. Does that mean there'll be a murder tonight that replicates the one she's about to shoot?

She finds herself eyeing Jaden in his black, graduation-gown costume, holding a rubber skull mask in one gloved hand and looking pretty scary. His brown eyes pierce her soul as he stares fixedly without blinking. She looks away, shivering. What is it with Jaden anyway? Kristen wasn't far off when she accused him of getting too much into the killer role.

Donovan is almost unrecognizable in stylish designer clothes and no hat, his hair slicked down with gel so it looks like he has bangs instead of his usual frizzled curls. He touches his sticky hair and grimaces.

"I'm having second thoughts about this, Cass. Why don't you play this part? We both know more guys watch horror films than girls."

Blonde hair tied into a pony tail that drops down her back, Kristen folds her arms across her chest, reeking of smugness. "Yeah, Cass. You be-ing in the film will *really* elevate my acting to stellar proportions."

Diego whispers, "Kristen." His tone is chastising, but Cassie ignores them both to focus on Donovan.

"We both decided this film wouldn't pander to those guys who like see-ing girls stalked and killed. You agreed with me on that. Besides, our odds are better at festivals if we don't give into those sexist clichés."

Donovan looks crestfallen. "What about Diego?"

Diego smiles, his wavy black hair, smooth skin, and soft features looking especially handsome beneath the moody overhead streetlight.

"I die later, remember, Mr. Writer?" He playfully shoves Donovan to show he's not being mean.

Donovan looks disappointed. Then he snaps his fingers. "Jaden could do it, right, Jaden? You took more acting classes than I did."

Without the ever-present hoodie, Jaden's cornrows catch Cassie's eye. They wrap down and around the back of his head, perfectly twined, not a single hair out of place, and their attractiveness belies his intimidating facial expression.

"I only took those classes 'cause my mom thought it would help my shyness. It didn't. 'Sides, I like being the guy in the mask."

Kristen snorts. "Yeah, too much. I bet you stalk girls around the neighborhood too, don't you?"

Jaden bows his head in embarrassment.

Cassie knows she must regain control. "Enough. You're it, Donovan, for the reason I gave you at school. Remember?"

He hesitates.

Kristen eyes her suspiciously. "What reason?"

"Never mind," Cassie replies with barely a glance her way. "So, D-Boy, how about it?"

That adorable shy smile slides across his mouth, replacing the look of trepidation and lighting up his face like he's a work of fine art.

"I'll give it my best shot."

Relieved, she grins and nudges him toward the backyard. "You and Jaden can practice the stalk and kill while I get set up with William and Baxter and our stars." She hopes her tone is firm, but not condescending, as she indicates Kristen and Diego, who both look pleased by her use of the term "stars."

"You're a terrific actor, Donovan," Jaden assures him. "This'll be fun."

Under her breath, Kristen mutters, "I bet."

Donovan ignores Kristen to focus on Jaden. "For you, maybe. I'm gonna die, remember?"

It's clearly a joke, but Cassie shudders, like a ghost passed through her. "Don't even joke like that."

Jaden lowers his gaze to the ground and loses the easiness of a moment before.

"Sorry," Donovan says, tossing off a shrug. "Come on, Jaden, let's rehearse."

He heads toward the dimly lit path that leads into the backyard. Jaden jogs after him and Cassie waves at the other actors to follow her across the lawn toward William and the camera setup.

Jaden catches up to Donovan near to where the path vanishes beneath a wooden backyard gate.

"You okay, Donovan?"

Donovan stops and turns, glancing up and down the darkened street. Sporadic streetlights offer scant illumination. Several parked cars look like slumbering dinosaurs and the "normalness" of the quiescent two-story homes sends a shiver down his back. The air is still and warm and there're no sounds except those made by his cast and crew.

"That murder last night has me spooked."

"That's life in LA. Lotta crazy people."

Donovan doesn't like Jaden's casual, almost callous tone. He studies him a moment, causing the other boy to look away.

"You, uh, ready to rehearse?" Jaden doesn't make eye contact, and his monotone voice gives away nothing.

Donovan nods, shaking off the chilling sensation that's crept over him. "Yeah."

Jaden points to a particular paving stone just in front of the gate. "Remember to hit that mark exactly so I can come at you from behind this tree"—he indicates the tree behind him—"and then the camera angle will be perfect."

Donovan studies the paving stones. They all look alike to him, but Jaden's finger clearly points to one in particular.

"That photographic memory is amazing."

Cassie absently twists strands of her hair into knots as William removes the camera from its tripod. He's been shooting the house and the surrounding neighborhood—"establishing shots" to set up this new location for viewers. He's a master at making the ordinary look sinister as hell. She's anxious to move on to the kill, but can't control the butterflies swarming in her stomach.

Could they be setting up another innocent person for death?

"You sure you want all Steadicam, before I strap it on?"

William's deep voice cuts into her thoughts like a butcher knife through a chunk of meat, and she nearly jumps in fright, her heart leaping into overdrive.

"Yes." Drawn back into the art of filmmaking, she wonders if he has an objection he's not voicing. "For stalk and kills, I think it works best. Do you have a different idea?"

He shakes his head. "No, I agree. Especially when you cut in shots from the drone. Both will be moving cameras, so it'll match."

"Exactly."

He peeks out from behind his bangs, offering a bashful grin.

"I was hoping you hadn't changed your mind because I already adjusted the light positions for Steadicam."

She studies him beneath the atmospheric lighting. He's always kept his hair long in front and short in back, more often than not hiding his eyes behind those bangs. Donovan told her that William does this because he prefers not to be noticed, and that's why he's so good at cinematography. While in his "invisible" mode, he watches others through his hair and pictures the best camera angles to use when filming them.

When he asked to be the director of photography on this film, Mr. K approved that request immediately. Cassie and Donovan had already discussed the DP position and hoped Mr. K would give them William, or Asher, who's almost as talented.

Cassie and William had never worked together on a film prior to this one. Thoughts of the real killer flee her mind as she considers how well he can already foresee her preferred camera set ups for particular scenes. They'd discussed using Steadicam for this sequence, even though it's not a stalk scene, but hadn't established the choice. Somehow, William figured out that she *had* confirmed it in her mind and set the stage accordingly.

Returning the grin, she says, "I think I want you as DP on all my films."

He basks in the glow of her compliment, possibly blushing too, but it's too shadowy for her to tell. To cover the awkward moment, he squats down to grab the Steadicam unit and she helps him strap it on. It's composed of a harness that wraps around his shoulders and back, with a belt connecting it together at the waist. She grabs the metal control arms and assists with their attachment, after which he locks the camera in place.

He looks like a steel-armed cyborg, but she loves how he can walk or run with the camera and the image doesn't jiggle in the slightest. In her mind, the Steadicam is the key piece of equipment for building suspense in their stalking scenes.

Baxter jogs over, remote in one hand and bag of chips in the other. He tosses off a loopy smile and pushes up his sagging glasses with the hand holding the chips.

"Drone is ready to stalk and shoot."

"Awesome." Cassie loves Baxter's drone footage, too. It gives the film a highly professional look.

Asher holds a camera that's smaller than William's and isn't attached to a Steadicam because in the film within the film, his character doesn't use one. He wears a ratty-looking polo shirt and cargo shorts because his cameraman character doesn't care much for fashion, seeing as he's never on camera himself. He winks at William, who's ratty attire he's mimicking.

William shoves his long bangs off his face. "Don't make us cameramen look bad, Asher."

Asher salutes. "Yes, sir!"

William grins.

Cassie scopes out her other actors for any last-minute costume, hair, or makeup needs. Seeing none, she announces, "Okay, everyone into position. Just like we rehearsed, guys. Ashley is directing the stalk and kill and Pedro is her script supervisor. Do you need another run-through?

Smirking, Diego raises the pad of paper and pen he's been holding. "I'm ready to write down all her mistakes."

Kristen scowls at both of them. "We know our jobs, Cassie. Let's shoot it."

She struts off to her starting mark while Cassie leads Baxter over near

Donovan and Jaden, who silently await their cue. Other crew members from Mr. K's class adjust lights and one boy holds out the boom mic on a long pole, ready to capture sound while keeping the microphone out of the shot.

"Okay, everyone in place," Cassie announces. "This is the master, so we're running the whole scene."

The crew members scurry to their assigned spots while Jaden slips the mask over his head. The skull face is pasty white with realistic-looking teeth, and eye holes for the actor to see through. A crew member hands him a large, gleaming prop knife, easily long enough to pierce Donovan's torso. Jaden presses on the tip and the blade retracts into the handle. When he lets go, the silver blade pops back out. He offers a thumbs up to Cassie and trots down the path around the corner of the house out of sight.

Cassie waves to Donovan. He strides across the lawn and enters the house, closing the front door behind him. Kristen stands before a dummy video monitor while Asher points his camera at the front door. Diego hovers behind Kristen, watching the front door, notebook out and ready.

William aims his Steadicam at the door, keeping Kristen, Diego, and Asher in the shot. Cassie listens through a headset and gazes intently at a monitor set off to one side to view what William's camera is capturing. She studies the camera shot of Kristen, Diego, Asher, and the front door. Everything looks good.

"Roll camera."

"Camera rolling," William replies. "Speed."

Cassie calls out, "Action!"

Kristen, playing Ashley, stares into the dummy monitor and says to Asher, "Roll camera."

Asher adjusts the video camera in his hands. "Camera rolling. Speed."

Kristen glances at the front door. "Action!"

The front door opens and Donovan, playing a nameless student victim, sticks his head out, as though expecting someone to be there. When he sees the porch is empty, he steps outside onto the lawn, glowering at the dimly lit front yard.

"I know someone's out here. I heard you. We're trying to work in here, so get lost."

From around the side of the house comes Jaden's muffled voice, "Come and make me."

Donovan's face turns stormy. He steps onto a paving stone path that winds around the house to the back. Both Asher and William track him in master shots, capturing all of the action within the frame. The "angry" Donovan stalks toward the corner of the house, Asher and William right with him, William always keeping Asher in his wide shot.

Just as Donovan turns the corner of the house, Jaden, wearing the skull mask, leaps from behind a tree to grab him around the throat so quickly that Donovan can't even cry out. He struggles, fists flailing, but Jaden whips up the knife and plunges it into his chest.

Kristen calls out, "Cut!"

The actors freeze, the hilt of the blade pressed against Donovan's upper torso, while Asher lowers his prop camera.

"Cut!" Cassie's voice pierces the night like a red alert claxon.

William stops filming as Jaden pulls back the knife. The blade pops out with a *click,* but Jaden doesn't take off the mask. Instead, he stares at Donovan as though wondering what it might feel like to really kill him.

Donovan gazes at the silent skull mask, where Jaden's shadowed eyes watch from within, and quickly turns away to face Cassie.

"That looked perfect, everyone," Cassie gushes, beaming.

Kristen strolls closer, Diego at her heels like a lapdog. "Of course, we were perfect."

"We'll do one more for safety and then shoot the closeups."

Looking relieved to be away from Jaden, who continues staring at him from within the mask, Donovan hurries to Cassie's side.

She notices Jaden watching them with a peculiar tilt of his head, as though she's some alien being he's never seen before. "You can take off the mask between takes, Jaden."

He doesn't say anything; just stares.

Kristen gives him an accusatory glare. "I think he adopted that method acting Mrs. K taught us about."

Cassie shudders as Jaden continues his behind-the-mask silent treatment.

"Guess so. Okay, everyone, back to one."

They scatter to their assigned spots, Donovan giving Jaden a wide berth as he heads back to the front door.

While the kids film five blocks away, Paisley Park basks in the faint glow of scattered light posts that produce small pools of illumination along a concrete path that appears to carve the well-kept grass into puzzle pieces. It's a small park with a play area for children and several benches set at various locations along the path for people who just want to relax and enjoy the serenity.

It's a warm spring night, but the park is devoid of life except for one desperate soul slumped on a wooden bench not far from a large deciduous tree in full spring bloom. The man's age is unclear due to the ravages of street life, but he's undoubtedly been homeless for some time. A frail, emaciated arm barely hidden beneath a threadbare shirtsleeve haltingly lifts a rumpled paper bag to his lips. The top of a bottle pokes out of the bag and he swigs the alcohol in deep, noisy gulps.

Behind the thick trunk of a tree twenty feet away lurks a tall figure wearing a mask and mechanic's overalls. In one hand, a large kitchen knife gleams beneath the moonlight.

The old man upends the bag, his head tilted back as far as possible as he slurps the final few drops trickling from the bottle. Lowering his head, he gazes bleary-eyed around him at the silent, empty park. His wrinkled, mottled skin looks pasty and diseased beneath the feeble glow of the overhead lamppost. Staggering to his feet, he stumbles back against the bench, tossing the bag away in his fear of falling. The bag strikes the concrete walkway, and the bottle within shatters. The sound of breaking glass angrily pierces the solitude.

The old man grips the back of the bench and manages to stay on his feet, but just barely. Steadying himself, he lurches forward, stumbling toward the tree with the thick trunk. Staggering as though the earth is rumbling beneath his poorly shod feet, he reaches out and slams his hand up against the bark of the tree just in time to avoid crumpling to the grass.

The figure lunges from behind the tree and slams a shoulder hard into the man, pressing him back against the trunk. The old man grunts in startled surprise, his rheumy eyes struggling to focus on the figure before him. Were he younger and not inebriated, he might have noticed that the mask worn by his assailant closely resembles that of Michael Myers, the psychopathic killer from the *Halloween* movies.

The man opens his mouth as though to speak, but before he can utter a word, the figure plunges a knife downward. The blade pierces the scrawny, sunken chest and sinks all the way in, propelled with sufficient force that its tip embeds itself within the tree trunk behind him.

The masked figure steps back as blood seeps from the old man's chest in a small stream, darkening the grass at the figure's booted feet. The man's eyes gradually glaze over as the masked figure tilts its head from side to side, admiring the macabre display it has created.

CHAPTER FOUR

STALKING CASSIE

CASSIE, WITH HELP FROM DONOVAN and Baxter, loads the last of the film equipment into the back of her dad's SUV. The rest of the cast and crew have already departed for home. Donovan's shirt has a ragged tear and sticky red Karo syrup coats his exposed chest, soaking his shirt and even his pants. He shivers as he gently places the Steadicam atop the other equipment and wraps it in a thick mover's blanket.

"That's everything," Baxter says, his voice sounding weary. "You better come inside and change, Donovan. Otherwise, my neighbors might call the cops."

Donovan shivers again. "I *am* cold. You used, like, three blood bags on me."

Baxter's eyes behind the thick lenses dance with mirth. "Hey, it's a horror film."

Cassie claps Donovan on the shoulder. "You do 'dead' really well, D-Boy."

"Very funny."

"I'm serious. That footage of you pinned to the house with Jaden admiring the kill is *so* good! I can't wait to get into the editing room."

Donovan nods. "Me too. Editing's my favorite part."

Cassie gives him a playful shove. "I think you should stick to acting. The camera loves you. Especially those hazel eyes. They practically sparkle."

"Trying to dump your partner already?" He pretends to look offended.

"No way. But you *do* look great on camera."

"Thanks."

Baxter picks up his drone from the sidewalk and cradles it lovingly. "You want me to stay with you, Cass, while he changes?"

Cassie glances around at the empty neighborhood. It's quiet and no one is in sight, which doesn't necessarily settle her nerves. Now that filming is over for the night, she's resumed wondering if something will happen out there. Something real. It's almost too horrifying to think about.

She studies the large tree behind her that separates Baxter's house from his neighbor's. It's the tree Jaden hid behind while stalking Donovan in the film. Is she being paranoid or did she spot just the slightest of movements behind that trunk? She shakes off her fear and offers Baxter a solid smile, calling up her own acting prowess to make it sincere.

"No, I'll be fine. Just don't take forever, D-Boy." She gives him an affectionate shove toward the house.

He grins and salutes. "Yes, Madam Director."

His good-natured humor almost puts her at ease as the boys head up the stone walkway toward the front door.

Baxter turns to Donovan. "I got another trivia question."

"Shoot."

"How many people who were connected to *The Exorcist* died during production?"

His cocky tone indicates he thinks he has a winner, but the watching Cassie knows better.

"Nine," Donovan answers without hesitation.

Baxter groans in disappointment. "And, sadly, you advance to double jeopardy."

Donovan laughs as they disappear into the house.

Cassie looks away from the closed front door to focus on the empty street. Occasional pools of street light punctuate the darkness and the houses look quiet. Too quiet, it seems to her, for a Saturday night. Not a partier herself, she wishes that someone on this street was having one. Music and laughter might soothe her soul and suppress her fears. But there's nothing.

She suddenly wishes she'd taken Baxter up on his offer.

Don't be paranoid. There's no one here but you.

She stares at a fancy mailbox across the street that's adorned with humorous artwork—a small dog grabbing the bag of a mailman. It's clearly hand-painted, conjuring memories of her mom, who would've loved it.

Gloria Stewart died when Cassie was seven, but she recalls that last hospital visit as though it were yesterday. Her vibrant, effervescent, fun-loving mother reduced to a shell of her former self, ravaged by brain cancer, lying beneath an oxygen tent fighting for the right to simply breathe.

Cassie had stood by her mother's bed drenched in tears of devastation and loss, her dad's strong arm wrapped tightly around her as he shed tears of his own.

She often wonders what her mom would think of how she's grown up and matured.

Would she be disappointed because I'm not a painter like her?

Even at age six, when she and Donovan first became friends, Cassie had a keen interest in everything that went bump in the night. But painting was never her forte. That was Donovan's talent even back then and her mother spent countless hours with him in her studio, teaching him everything she knew.

Had she been disappointed in Cassie? Not that she ever displayed. She'd always sat eagerly beside her daughter to watch the old black and white Universal horror flicks and even the classic Hammer films starring Peter Cushing and Christopher Lee, never once even hinting that she wasn't having the best time ever. Donovan was often there too, but mostly it was just her and Mom. Her dad said those movies scared him too much to watch with them. That always struck her as funny, coming from a cop.

Might she have turned out more like the other girls at school if she hadn't been raised by a single dad? Would she be all aflutter at every cute boy who gave her the eye, and stress out over her appearance twenty-four seven like all the girls on social media seem to do? Considering how happy she is with her present self, she sincerely hopes not.

Crack!

She freezes.

That sounded like someone stepping on a twig.

She spins around in a circle, taking in Baxter's house and the neighborhood with a careful sweep of her studied gaze.

Nothing.

Then why do I feel so sure someone's watching me?

Once again, she scans the street and surrounding homes. Most of the houses are two-story, like Baxter's, with gabled upper floor windows—some glowing with warm light, others dark as the grave. In her horror-film-fueled-imagination, she conjures all manner of stalkers lurking behind every tree and hedge, waiting for just the right moment to plunge a knife into her wildly thumping heart.

And yet, it's not her imagination sending alarms bells clanging in her head.

Someone *is* watching her.

For real.

But from where?

Footsteps squishing against grass cause her to whirl in surprise. Coming at her from Baxter's enormous tree is a figure wearing a Michael Myers-type mask and wielding a massive kitchen knife!

Cassie gasps and turns to run, slamming into the SUV and cracking her knee hard against the fender. Whimpering as pain ricochets throughout her body, she glances back to see the figure stalking toward her. She stumbles around the SUV and into the street, limping as her knee aches and her heart hammers like gunfire. The footsteps increase their pace as they hit the pavement, moving into a run while she increases her stride. But the throbbing in her knee slows her speed to a moderate limp and the slap of heavy shoes against asphalt from behind grows closer every second.

She's moments away from entering the front yard of the house directly across from Baxter's when a siren rips a single note into the night and bright blue light suddenly blinds her. She stumbles to a halt, nearly tripping against the curb, as a police car screeches to a stop and her dad leaps from the driver's seat, gun out and pointed behind her.

Almost fainting from relief, her breathing ragged, she pivots to see her father step toward the figure.

"Drop the knife now!" His deep voice booms through the night like cannon fire.

The figure freezes in place as though glued, throwing both arms into the air without hesitation. The knife drops from one hand and strikes the pavement where it … bounces?

Cassie gazes in amazement at the bouncing knife, her fear instantly replaced by disbelief as the rubber blade bends when it strikes the asphalt and then flips over to land on its side.

Her dad's young partner, Officer Delgado, is also out of the car, gun pointed at the unmoving figure.

Edward steps closer. "Don't even think of moving. Delgado, cuff him."

Officer Delgado holsters his weapon and detaches handcuffs from his belt. They gleam beneath the streetlight as he gingerly approaches the figure.

From beneath the mask, the figure says, "But I—"

"Not a word," Edward barks, his gun aimed squarely at the figure's chest. "Hands behind your back. Now!"

The figure complies without hesitation. As Delgado, who's considerably shorter and less thick around the torso than the masked guy, slaps the cuffs on him, Cassie wonders why the figure's voice sounds so familiar.

"Take off the mask, Delgado," Edward continues, his weapon still up and ready, "but carefully. We don't want to compromise the forensics."

Delgado pulls a latex glove from his belt and slips it on. He steps forward and gently tugs the mask up and over the figure's head.

Cassie gasps in stunned surprise. "Robert!"

Edward finally lowers his weapon but doesn't holster it as Cassie limps toward Robert, whose large frame—encased in baggy overalls—and haughty face look shrunken with fear.

"What the hell are you doing, Robert?"

Robert nods toward the knife at his feet. "It's f-f-fake," he says, deep voice trembling. "I-I swear."

Edward finally replaces his gun in the holster and eyes both of them. "We can see that. I take it this is the Robert who's been hitting on you all year?"

Cassie nods, unable to take her eyes off Robert. His drawn face doesn't look so handsome now, but his terror is genuine. She can practically feel him trembling.

"Yeah. I fired him today because he kissed me against my will."

Edward squints at Robert in anger, but turns to her, eyebrows raised. "What did you do?"

"Kneed him in the balls, like you taught me."

Edward nods, looking grim as he studies the trembling Robert, who acts so different from the cocky jerk of just hours before who'd made an unwanted pass at her.

"Well, this knife might be fake, but the one he stuck into an old man at the park was very real."

Robert gasps, his eyes the size of golf balls. "The hell?"

Delgado steps forward. "You're under arrest, kid. I'll read you your rights at the car and it *will* be recorded."

He points to the small body camera attached to his uniform.

Robert looks like he's about to faint. Even within the dim pools cast by overhead streetlights, his face looks sickly white.

"This was just a prank on Cass. I don't know nothing about some guy in the park. Shit, I found this mask and stuff on the hood of my car!"

Cassie tosses her dad a bewildered look, but he just nods to Delgado, who takes Robert by one arm and leads him to the squad car, its twirling light enveloping them in a ghastly blue glow.

Over his shoulder, Robert calls out in desperation, "I didn't mean nothing by it, Cass! I was just mad, okay?"

Delgado shoves Robert into the back seat of the squad car before he can say anything more.

Donovan sprints out the front door, Baxter in tow. Donovan's back in his regular clothes, but his plaid shirt is open, flapping in the breeze, as though he spotted what was happening before he had time to button it.

"Cass, are you all right?" Despite the short run from the house to the street, he's already winded.

"I'm fine. Robert was pranking me."

"Then why was he arrested?" Baxter holds yet another bag of chips in hand, but his eyes look eerily magnified behind his large glasses.

Cassie turns to her dad. "Do you really think he killed someone?"

Donovan flinches and Baxter stops in mid-chew.

Edward eyes them all, looking more distressed than Cassie can remember seeing him in a long time.

"Somebody wearing that mask sure as hell did. We need to get him down to the station. Go straight home and take Donovan with you." He faces Donovan. "Your mother working another all-nighter?"

Donovan nods.

"I'll text her and explain why you're staying at my place again tonight.

Lock the doors and windows and don't open for anyone. Baxter, you do the same. Whatever's going on seems to revolve around your film."

Baxter's chubby cheeks sag with fear, the bag of chips forgotten. "Yes, sir."

Edward gives Cassie a quick look of encouragement before trotting back to his cruiser. He climbs into the driver's seat and closes the door. The siren engages and the car roars off down the quiet street amidst swirling flashes of blue light.

Cassie feels like a bus slammed into her, and not just because of her throbbing knee. Robert, a murderer? It doesn't seem possible.

Baxter stares at her in disbelief. "Robert killed someone?"

Donovan fumbles with the buttons on his shirt. "I knew he was a jerk, but I never thought he was that bad."

Cassie tries to wrap her mind around tonight's events. "Me, either."

There's a long moment of silence between them. The crunch of Baxter's teeth on a handful of chips breaks the spell.

"You heard your dad," Donovan says to Cassie. "Let's get out of here. See you tomorrow, Baxter."

Baxter nods and waddles up the walk to his house without another word. The door opens and then the house swallows him up. The quiet is so intense Cassie can hear the deadbolt click into place.

Donovan looks concerned. "You look spooked, Cass. Want me to drive?"

She shakes her head. "No, I'm good."

She steps up into the driver's seat while he scuttles around to climb into the passenger side. Cassie starts the SUV and, with one final glance at the tree Robert hid behind, drives off into the night, wondering just how long he'd been there before making his move.

CHAPTER FIVE

SETTING A TRAP FOR THE KILLER

As Cassie lies in bed that night, she focuses more on the whys and wherefores of Robert being a killer than the frightful scare she received at having been stalked. That lack of emotional residue from the attack bothers her more than anything else. Every girl she knows would be wound up in knots over the incident, but all she can do is consider the possibility that Robert killed that man in the park.

As far back as she can remember, she's always been less emotional than other girls and wonders for the umpteenth time if being raised by her dad might be a contributing factor. Never one to wear his emotions on his sleeve, Edward has always modeled clear thinking for handling every situation she's ever faced. She considers her rational nature a net positive when it comes to a career in Hollywood, especially because she has Donovan by her side and he's the emotional one. Should she try for a better balance within herself? That question whirls around in her head as she finally drops into a light sleep.

When she enters her kitchen the next morning, she finds Donovan at the breakfast table sipping steaming hot chocolate from a mug shaped like a movie camera. His brown hair is wildly askew and he's clearly tried to stuff it all up under a purple velvet fedora, without significant success. It pokes out everywhere in an Albert Einstein sort of way, and his clothes are more mismatched than she can ever recall.

He's actually wearing a baggy short-sleeve pink polka dot dress shirt that's two sizes too big for him and even baggier camouflage cargo shorts that drop well below his knees and, she's certain, are being held in place with one of her dad's belts. He's always kept some spare articles of clothing in the hall closet for times when his mom works the night shift, but today he clearly doesn't care how he looks.

Normally, she'd razz him over his appearance, but not today. Her auburn hair is more disheveled than his, though she did brush it rather extensively and used quite a bit of detangle spray (with little result), and her mix of jeans and a Film Club tee shirt sure won't get her the Best Dressed Senior award in the yearbook either.

Having tabled her self-reflection on emotion versus rationality while brushing her hair, she's decided to focus again on the murders and Robert's possible involvement. Even as a freshman, he was handsome and cocky, flirting with every girl he saw. He lorded his muscles over the unathletic boys, but he was never one to pick fights or get in anyone's face when challenged.

As she absently heads for the coffee pot, she recalls seeing him and his parents at Open House, vividly remembering (because she mentioned it to her dad) how Robert's father seemed to hit on female teachers and parents right in front of his wife! Like father like son, maybe, but can arrogance and an overactive libido lead someone to murder?

Donovan looks up from his mug of chocolate. "It's a good thing I keep extra clothes here, huh?"

She grunts while pouring herself some coffee. She vaguely hears him speaking; her thoughts remain fixed on Robert.

"Otherwise I'd be running around naked like Christian Bale in American Psycho," Donovan adds. "With a chainsaw."

Cassie grunts again and sips her coffee.

Donovan waves his arms like he's flagging down planes at the airport. "Earth to Cass?"

She slowly becomes aware of his waving arms and turns her attention to him. "Sorry. What did you say?"

"Nothing. Bad joke. No word from Pop?"

She shakes her head as she lowers herself into a chair at the table directly across from him.

"I just don't believe Robert could… That would mean he killed the other guy too. He'd have to be psycho."

Donovan scowls. "He *has* been stalking you all year."

"Yeah, but random murders?"

"He sexually assaulted you." He reeks with pent-up anger.

She eyes him for a moment, noting his stiff posture and the downward turn of his mouth.

"It was just a kiss, Donovan, and I'm the one who assaulted him. No, it doesn't add up."

The front door opens and closes, and they both stiffen. When her dad enters, he's accompanied by an attractive woman dressed in stylish business attire, low-heeled shoes, and carrying a small handbag over one shoulder.

Cassie leaps to her feet. "Marisol!" She glances from the woman to her dad. "Are you guys back together?"

Edward clears his throat, clearly uncomfortable. "No. Detective Santiago has been assigned to the horror film killer case. She needs to ask you both some questions."

Cassie and Donovan exchange a look of confusion. Marisol had been Edward's fiancé, but they broke up suddenly last year and Edward hasn't spoken of her since.

Marisol looks just as beautiful as ever with her curly black hair cut short in back but fuller on the sides and top, accentuating her light brown skin and vibrant brown eyes. Cassie has always admired how Marisol managed the perfect mix of feminine and professional, beautiful and stylish while projecting a dead-serious demeanor that clearly indicates she's not to be messed with by anyone.

"Good to see you again, Cass," Marisol says, her voice soft, yet firm. "You too, Donovan. Still just friends?"

Cassie and Donovan nod simultaneously. The level of awkwardness could be cut with a knife.

Without even looking at Marisol, Edward says, "Detective Santiago knows about your film and has some questions."

Cassie nods, having known this moment would arrive.

They can't shut down our film, can they?

Edward gestures toward the door. "Let's sit in the living room."

He gestures for Marisol to go first and then the kids. Nerves thrumming with anxiety, Cassie follows Donovan while her dad brings up the rear.

The Stewart living room is neat and tidy, her mom's nature paintings on the walls along with several commemorative plaques with Edward's name on them—commendations from the mayor and Chief of Police for Outstanding Community Policing.

Cassie and Donovan sit on the big comfortable couch, but the adults remain standing, one at either end of the spacious room. Their behavior is almost weirder than what happened with Robert.

"So," Marisol begins, her tone clipped and practiced, "Officer Stewart filled me in on this movie you're making and I have some questions."

The formality between these two adults who not so long ago were headed for marriage is disconcerting. For now, however, Cassie decides to focus on the matter at hand.

"I've thought a lot since last night, and I don't think Robert's the killer, Mar—Detective. I have a feeling you don't either." She feels unsettled calling someone she thinks of as a surrogate mother by her job title.

Marisol offers what could be a slight smile, but it vanishes as quickly as it arrived. "Sharp as ever, I see. No, I don't. The forensics are still being gathered, but what we do know doesn't add up. Robert's fingerprints are on the murder weapon, but in the wrong direction."

Donovan sits forward on the couch, elbows planted on his knees. "What do you mean?"

"Run to the kitchen and bring me a large cutting knife, will you, Donovan?"

He hurries out of the room. While he's gone, Cassie studies her father and Marisol, who have not made eye contact once since they entered the house. She can't imagine a reason for them to not even look at each other, and that troubles her. They were patrol partners who fell in love, dated for two years, and planned to marry. When Marisol became a detective, everything fell apart between them.

Donovan returns carrying a large kitchen knife that looks like the real version of what Jaden used in the film last night. He hands it off to Marisol and then retakes his place on the couch. His presence calms Cassie, as always.

Marisol grips the knife with her forefinger near the gleaming stainless steel blade. "Robert picked up the knife like this, forefinger close to the blade, as though he was about to cut a steak. The angle of the entry wound in the victim indicates that the knife was plunged in at a slight downward angle. To do that, the killer would have to clutch the knife this way."

She switches the knife so that now her index finger is near the back end of the handle, away from the blade. Cassie and Donovan nod their understanding, and Marisol lays the knife down on the marble coffee table.

Cassie leans forward. "How did Robert's fingerprints get on the knife?"

"He said he found the costume, mask, and two knives on the hood of his car with a note that read, 'Get her back.' He said he picked up the real knife to check it out and then threw it into a nearby trash can. The other items he kept, as you know."

Cassie considers this information for a moment before addressing her dad. "Do you believe him, Dad?

Edward shuffles his feet, but maintains eye contact with Cassie. "I didn't interrogate him. Detective Santiago did. You know him better than we do. What's your opinion?"

"Robert's a jerk and thinks he's all that, but I don't think he's a killer."

Edward's eyes shift to Donovan.

"I can't stand him, but I agree with Cass," Donovan replies. "He's an arrogant showoff, but I don't think he has the guts to kill someone."

"So, that brings us to your film," Marisol says. "It seems to be the eye of the storm. Tell me, how did you get your script and location schedule to cast and crew?"

"Email," answer Cassie and Donovan simultaneously.

Marisol forces back a smile at their synchronicity. "Did you encrypt it?"

Cassie eyes Donovan for a moment. "No, we didn't think we needed to."

"Then either of your emails could've been hacked."

"I guess," Donovan says, sounding dubious.

"Have you noticed anyone you didn't recognize watching the filming?"

They shake their heads.

Cassie posits the idea she's been considering since Friday. "You think someone is copycatting our story?"

"It would be a pretty big stretch to think otherwise," Marisol answers matter-of-factly. "You're filming a story about kids making a movie where someone is copycatting the killings in their movie. It's just too coincidental to be a coincidence."

Looking down at the carpet rather than at Marisol, Edward says, "So, what do you want them to do, stop filming?"

Her heart pounding, Cassie practically leaps off the couch. "Dad!"

Marisol focuses on Cassie and Donovan, her tone crisp and focused. "No, but I do want to try an experiment. So far, the killer has struck on the same nights you killed someone in your movie. When is the next kill scene?"

Donovan peeks out from beneath his fedora. "Tonight. We trade off directing duties and today's my day. We're doing a killing from the movie *Scream*."

Marisol nods. "Then we can expect the real killer, if as we suspect, it isn't Robert, to strike tonight."

Edward interjects, "Why not move that kill scene to another night?"

Marisol glowers at the interruption.

Cassie furrows her brows in confusion. "Why do that?"

Edward clears his throat again but fixes his eyes on Cassie, clearly avoiding Marisol's penetrating gaze.

"If the killer got your shooting schedule online and is following it, he'll plan to kill someone tonight the same way you do and will probably make the attempt even if you change things up, because he won't know you moved that scene. *But*, if he's observing the shoot, he'll know you didn't film that kill and might not do one of his own. At least, it will give us a clue how the killer is getting his ideas."

Marisol looks impressed, gazing at Edward with a touch of admiration. "That's the kind of thinking that would have made passing the detective exam a breeze."

Edward finally makes eye contact with her, his body taut, controlled anger in his squint. "Thanks. But, as I told you at the time, *Detective*, I like being a neighborhood cop."

Cassie nods her understanding of Edward's explanation.

"If the killer is secretly observing you," Marisol puts in, "rather than having already read the script, it might be easier to flush him out. I was going to suggest you change tonight's killing to a different one from your script, but instead I'd like you to follow Officer Stewart's plan."

Frustrated at the childishness of the adults in barely speaking to each other, Cassie turns to Donovan. "You're the director."

Donovan looks rattled. "It's… sure, it's okay with me."

"But don't tell anyone of the change until the very moment you're supposed to shoot that scene," Edward adds, focusing on Donovan.

Marisol frowns. "This is my case, Officer."

Edward folds his arms across his chest. "Sorry. *Detective.*"

Marisol pulls her probing gaze away from him and fixes it on the teens.

Anger wells up in Cassie about the discourteous way her dad is being treated, but before she can comment, Marisol continues in that commanding tone she's always had when embroiled in a case.

"We'll have officers combing the neighborhood around your location. The other killings have all been within a four-block radius of your filming sites. I want you both to keep my number in your phones. If you see or hear anything suspicious during your shoot, text me at once."

She reaches into the pocket of her slacks and extracts some business cards, handing one each to Cassie and Donovan.

"Sure, Mar—uh, Detective," Donovan stammers, taking the card between thumb and forefinger.

Cassie gazes at her father intensely, but he avoids making eye contact.

Marisol adds, "I'll be at the station today examining Robert's computer files for any contacts with people who might be the killer. I'll see myself out."

She turns and strides from the room without another word. The front door opens and closes, and all that remains is an awkward silence and the business card in Cassie's hand. She stares at the silent Edward, awaiting an explanation.

"Don't ask." He strides angrily from the room.

"What was that all about?" Donovan asks, his expression troubled. "I never asked why they broke up, but that was beyond weird."

Cassie feels embarrassed that she's never told him. "Marisol wanted Dad to take the detective exam when she did, so they could still be partners, but he refused."

Anger flashes across Donovan's hazel eyes like lightning. "He's the kind of guy who gives cops a good name. Everybody in the neighborhood loves him. What's wrong with that?"

"Nothing, except Marisol got mad and dumped him, from what little Dad told me."

Donovan shakes his head in disgust. "And they say us kids can't handle relationships."

She nods, troubled by the entire episode.

Cassie's backyard teems with acting students from school who play extras in the obligatory teen party scene, which features a number of possible murder suspects. They mill about wearing casual summer attire and drinking punch from red plastic cups. Flower beds blooming in red, yellow, and blue line the inside of the fence and a large rectangle of grass adorns the center, flanked all around by cobbled paving stones.

Delicious-smelling hotdogs sizzle on a barbecue grill sheltered under a wide overhang and several tables litter the lawn, their large shade umbrellas angled toward the warm afternoon sun. A six-foot foldout table sits beside the sliding glass door into the house, displaying a large cooler, red cups, and piles of snacks in colorful bags.

Cassie and Donovan stand near the backyard gate. She's observing everything for last minute changes while he reviews shot sheets.

Near the snacks table, William brushes his brown hair aside to peer through the camera lens at the milling crowd, adjusting the tripod to capture random moments that could be used as cutaways.

Baxter hovers by the table grabbing chips and shoving them into his mouth, at the same time stuffing snack bags into his fanny pack. Olivia chats with Diego, while Asher sits at the makeup table under the expert ministrations of Mrs. K.

She finishes highlighting the area around his eyes.

"Thanks, Mrs. K."

"You're most welcome, Asher," she replies, clearly pleased with her work. "A handsome boy like you needs only a few touches to highlight your cheeks and eyes."

Asher beams at the compliment.

Kristen ceases her conversation with one of the extras, roughly snatches Diego's hand and drags him away from the fawning Olivia, who sighs dramatically, drawing the attention of a group of girls ogling Diego.

Mrs. K strides over to them. She's dressed in her Principal Loomis-style pantsuit and tosses Diego a "look," as though she's about to give him detention.

"I hope you're not letting personal drama affect your performance, Diego. Flirting is best left off the set."

Diego flinches, clearly offended. "I wasn't flirting."

Mrs. Ketchum turns abruptly to face Kristen. "Are you ready?

"Yes."

Mrs. Ketchum leads Kristen toward William, leaving a sulking Diego to trail after them like a chastised little brother.

"William, do me a favor and check how her makeup looks through the camera."

"Sure Mrs. K." William gestures for Kristen to step in front of the camera and he adjusts the eyepiece to peer through. He tosses out a thumbs up and Mrs. K flashes Kristen a broad smile.

Cassie shakes her head at all the behind-the-scenes drama.

Donovan glances at the time on his phone. "We're right on schedule."

She offers a casual grin. "That's because we have a very good director."

"Thanks."

They're both dressed in typically casual style but, she has to admit, Donovan's quirky attire screams "stereotype of talented auteur!" He wears purple shorts, a red silk shirt that hugs his torso in places that continually draw her eye, and a red fedora.

She frowns at something and he turns to look. Jaden stands off by himself in one corner of the yard wearing the black gown and skull mask, staring at everyone, not moving.

"I wish he'd take that thing off. It gives me the creeps, especially since I know he's scoping you out." Donovan's voice is tinged with suspicion.

Cassie punches him on the arm. "You sound like a jealous teen from one of those stupid TV shows."

He grunts, glancing once more at Jaden. He tries a smile and a wave, but Jaden continues to perform the perfect impression of a wax statue.

"I admit he creeps me out, too," Cassie admits in a low voice. Leaning into his ear, she whispers, "I wonder how he'll react when he finds out we're not doing the kill scene."

He shrugs. "I don't know, but between him and Robert, this shoot seems to attract weirdos."

Cassie nudges him. "Speaking of which…"

Ron Warner, decked out in a loud blue sports jacket and fancy filigree scarf draped around his neck, saunters in their direction.

"Oh, great," Donovan mutters. "The King Creep himself."

Sporting a smug expression, Warner stops before them as though presenting himself for an academy award.

"Mr. Warner," Donovan offers in his calmest tone, "you're early. Your call time isn't till three and it's only one."

Warner tips his porkpie hat, revealing heavily greased hair slicked back Dracula style, and offers an obsequious smile.

"I just thought I'd drop by and watch you talented kids at work." He addresses both of them, but his gaze remains fixed on Cassie, who frowns in return.

Donovan steps protectively in front of her. "Thanks."

Warner gives him a cursory once over, as though sizing him up for a wardrobe fitting.

"You know, Donovan, your ragamuffin style of dress might have been in vogue thirty years ago, but if you want to make it in Hollywood today, you should dress to impress, as they say. Unless you're too poor to afford better clothes."

Cassie stiffens with anger and opens her mouth to issue a scathing retort, but Donovan's steady hand on her arm stops her.

"Mr. Warner, I purposely buy my clothes at thrift stores because that's my style," he explains calmly, "and no, I would never go into a job interview dressed like this, so you don't need to be concerned. In fact, you don't need to say anything else for the rest of the day except your lines."

Cassie guffaws in open-mouthed shock as Donovan gazes firmly at Warner and doesn't look the least bit intimidated.

Warner huffs indignantly. "I was just trying to be helpful. You kids today think you know everything. I'll be in my trailer having a drink. Let me know when you need me."

He starts off at an exaggerated strut past the refreshment table and on toward the tables and chairs.

"Trailer?" Cassie asks, confused.

Warner stops and, with a smarmy smile, points to a solitary table set off by itself in the farthest corner of the yard, umbrella shading the lone chair from the sun.

"As the veteran member of the cast, I require my privacy."

He stalks off past groups of laughing, chatting teens. Cassie notices Asher standing to one side filming Warner on his phone as the elder actor plants himself at his "trailer" table. He slips a metal flask from inside his jacket pocket and unscrews the top. He holds it out and grins before taking a long, exaggerated swig.

Cassie eyes Donovan. "That drink better be the punch we're serving."

He grunts. "Doesn't look like it. What is it with you attracting the weirdos?"

She points at her pale, dotted face, rimmed with loose strands of frizzy hair. "Must be the freckles."

He grins.

Asher approaches, holding his phone in one hand. "William said to tell you he's ready to shoot, Donovan."

Donovan nods and follows the other boy.

As they near William's camera setup, Asher directs Donovan's attention to Warner drinking from his flask in the corner.

"I don't trust that guy. He's still hitting on the girls and he's always sneaking drinks on set."

Donovan studies him. "Mr. K said it was your idea to bring him on this film."

Asher glances over quickly, but just as rapidly relaxes. "My mom loves the guy and since Mr. K knew him, I thought it might be good for the movie. I was wrong. Sorry, Donovan."

Donovan claps him on the back. "No worries. He may be a jerk and a pig, but his acting is good."

Asher chuckles, but something about the gesture strikes Donavan as off, like Asher is acting amused, but really isn't.

Definitely odd.

CHAPTER SIX

SOMEONE IS WATCHING

NIGHT HAS FALLEN AND CASSIE can't believe how quickly the day's shooting flew past. The party scene went off without a hitch despite the alcohol on Warner's breath. Cassie caught the smell of it whenever he'd wander into her space and lean in to offer an unwanted suggestion on how this actor or that one could "push her performance to the next level." The last thing she needs is a guy who got himself kicked out of Hollywood offering her advice, especially after the way he'd insulted Donovan earlier.

The filming has changed locations to the front of her single-story house. She takes a moment to observe Diego and Kristen rehearsing their lines near the front door. Donovan, William, and Asher are setting up a long tracking shot involving the camera on a dolly. Cassie turns to study Baxter. His fanny pack bulges with his ever-present chips as he maneuvers his drone up and over the houses, the streetlights reflecting off his huge glasses like beacons.

A movement at the corner of her eye causes her to glance toward the street. Warner lurks beneath a large tree, even though they'd sent him home two hours ago. What is he doing back at on set? Steeling herself, she strides across the expansive lawn, determined to be "diplomatic."

"Mr. Warner, you're done for the day. You can go home."

Okay, that came out kind of abrupt, but then she's never possessed Donovan's measured approach to handling other people.

Looking chillingly scary in the darkness beneath the tree, Warner reveals preternaturally white teeth, which, in combination with his slicked-back hair, adds to his Dracula look.

"I'm staying in a nearby hotel, so I moseyed on back to watch the kill scene."

She almost gags at the alcohol stench wafting out of his mouth like poisonous bug spray. It occurs to her that the time is fast approaching to announce the moving of the kill scene, and she *definitely* doesn't want Warner blabbing it to the rest of the crew.

Fortunately, she's saved when Donovan calls out, "Hey, Cass!"

She eyes Warner as best she can in the shadows, but can't make out his expression clearly enough to guess what he might be thinking.

"Excuse me." Jogging back to Donovan, she asks, "What's up?"

He points to a shadowy spot near the corner of the house where Jaden lurks, decked out in the full killer costume and apparently "psyching" himself up for the kill scene.

"You haven't told him, yet?"

"You're the director today, D-Boy. Besides, I thought we agreed to wait until after this tracking shot."

He sighs, obviously dreading Jaden's reaction as much as she is. "Yeah. I'll have him push the dolly."

"Good idea. That'll get him out of the mask." She freezes.

"What?"

"Someone's watching me."

"Someone's always watching you."

She's not amused by his joke, glancing around at the cast and crew. "I feel eyes on me."

Donovan extends his arm and sweeps it around. "Take your pick. Jaden, Warner, or Diego."

He points to Diego, who's staring at them but quickly pretends to focus on Kristen and Olivia, who appear to be arguing.

"And what's Warner doing back here, anyway?"

She ignores his question. "It's not any of them."

She spins around and scans the dark, shadowy street. The street circles past her home and wraps its way through rows of single-story homes before vanishing around the Thompson house at the corner.

She's about to turn back, but then she sees it.

A blur of movement.

Gray.

"There! Gray hoodie. It ducked behind the Thompson's house."

She glances over to determine if he saw the figure too, surprised to see anger brewing in his hazel eyes.

"I'm sick and tired of people messing with you," he announces, and his tone is as firm as she's ever heard from him.

Her breath freezes in her lungs when he strides forward toward the street.

She darts after him and grabs his arm. "What if he's the killer?"

He gazes at her long and hard, his handsome features set into a determined look. "I don't care." He shakes her hand loose and strides purposefully across the shadowy street.

She scrambles to follow, glancing side to side with trepidation, her heart hammering in her chest. It's one thing to direct a horror film, but altogether different to be living one.

The only sounds come from the cast and crew at her house behind them. Everywhere else there's nothing but a gloomy, suffocating silence. Cassie has to jog to keep pace with Donovan until he finally slows as he nears the Thompson house on the corner. It's a rambler-style one story sporting a terra cotta roof and desert-themed landscaping in the front yard.

It's also dark as the grave.

"Where did you see him?"

She points to a neatly trimmed hedge, easily six feet tall that shields the house from passersby on the adjacent street.

"He ducked behind the hedge, probably heading down Elm Street."

Donovan scans the area around the hedge and the two adjoining streets. There's no movement and no sound from any of the houses. He glances into the front yard of the Thompson home and reaches down to snatch up a fist-sized rock resting beside some succulents.

Cassie flanks him as they edge their way to the corner, tiptoeing to mask their presence in case hoodie guy is lurking on the other side of the hedge.

What if he has a knife?

She holds her breath as the corner looms closer, their soft footfalls sounding like explosions in her frenzied imagination.

Donovan stops and holds up a hand, and she halts beside him. His face is scrunched with concentration; they listen for any sounds or movement on the other side of the hedge. She hears nothing and studies his tight features for any indication that he might have, but he gives away nothing.

His entire body looks poised to strike, like a panther about to pounce on its prey. The hedge is made up of thick, twisting vines and tiny leaves, so tightly packed that no light even shines through. He waves her toward the corner. He leaps forward, rock poised to throw, and she's right beside him. Their feet land with a loud *slap* against the pavement and the adjoining Elm Street pops into view.

It's empty.

Not even a neighbor out walking his dog.

Releasing the breath she'd been holding in, she studies the houses carefully and senses that Donovan is doing the same. On the right are all two-story homes like Donovan's in that gabled, Cape Cod style that's so prevalent in the West Valley. On the left are single-story homes that look to have the same floorplan as hers.

Windows blaze with warm light spilling onto neatly trimmed lawns, and the streetlights offer pools of illumination every hundred feet. She scrutinizes each hedge and tree, even the picket fences that front many of the homes, but nothing moves, not even the thick foliage of city trees planted along the sidewalks.

She allows herself to breathe more normally, keenly aware of her wildly thumping heart. Donovan glances over, fear dancing across his beautiful eyes.

Lowering the rock to his side, he eyes her in the shadowy darkness. "The hoodie didn't look familiar?"

Cassie thinks a moment, then shakes her head. "C'mon, let's get back. We have that scene to shoot and then we'll tell everyone about the schedule change."

She takes his arm gently and tugs him back toward her house. He reluctantly follows, replacing the rock in its original spot as they scurry past the silent Thompson home.

"You need to text your dad and let him know what happened." His boyish voice is strained with fear.

She nods as they step out onto the asphalt and trot across the street toward the rest of the film crew.

"I will after you get the shot. He might be so spooked he'll shut us down just when we're ready to go."

His brows furrow. "All right, but stay close to me."

She nods and they rejoin the others.

To Cassie's intense relief, Jaden is only too happy to push the camera dolly, which means no killer mask for the time being. She tosses Donovan a quick thumbs up while he concentrates on setting up the scene.

Tracking shots are essential in horror films to help build suspense. This scene involves the camera—doubling as the killer's point of view—stalking Olivia as she leaves the party after failing in her attempt to seduce Diego's character, Pedro. She's angry and mutters to herself as she stalks down the sidewalk toward a car parked a block away.

Laying out the dolly tracks took over an hour and now the street looks like a railroad station, the tracks running adjacent to the sidewalk. William, Baxter, Jaden, and Donovan heft the cumbersome dolly onto the track and align the wheels so it will roll smoothly and (hopefully) not make unwanted squeaking noises that will wreak havoc with the film's audio track.

The dolly is a simple platform on wheels featuring a large handle at the rear for the operator to grip, while the cameraman stands on it with the camera. The boys manage to align the dolly so that it makes only occasional mouse-like squeaks at a couple of points along the track.

William sets the tripod onto the platform and clamps the feet into place so the camera won't tip over, and then Jaden carefully hands him the camera. Asher climbs aboard to help William lock down the camera and then William tosses Donovan a thumbs up. They're ready to shoot.

Jaden plants himself behind the dolly and grips the back rail firmly in both hands. Keeping a dolly, plus the weight of the cameraman, moving at a consistent pace takes strong arms and shoulders, not to mention legs. Jaden is small in stature, but he's so eager for the job that Donovan allows him to do it solo, despite the original plan to have Asher, who stayed behind to assist William, help him.

Donovan sits in a lawn chair before the monitor and places the headset over his ears, while Cassie stands to one side watching for any mistakes in the blocking. In the movie, the killer closes in on Olivia and just misses grabbing her as she reaches her car. She remains oblivious to how close she came to dying. The kill will happen later, in her character's backyard.

The tracking scene requires several takes to get just right, but finally Donovan looks satisfied, grinning at the performance of his cast and crew, heaping particular praise on Jaden, who maintained complete control over the heavy apparatus. The moody lighting by William and Asher is appropriately scary, and when Cassie stands by the monitor reviewing the footage alongside cast and crew, she gently squeezes Donavan's hand to congratulate him. The scene looks fantastic.

Despite not being needed any longer, Kristen and Diego have hung around to watch the rest of the filming. And Cassie is sorry to note, so has Warner. She knows they're all awaiting the "kill."

As the dolly's being folded up by William and Baxter, and Asher helps Jaden take the track apart, Cassie leans in to Donovan's ear. "It's time."

He peers out from beneath his fedora, meeting her gaze with a look of dismay. "Yeah."

He acts like he's headed for the electric chair as he approaches the small group huddled together against the chilly night air.

"Everyone, can I have your attention, please?"

Kristen and Diego cease their muted conversation as Warner and Olivia approach from different directions, Olivia giving the elder actor the evil eye. Having folded the dolly for storage, William, Baxter, Asher, and Jaden cease pulling apart the track and step closer to listen, Asher slipping out his phone and filming the group.

Donovan clears his throat. "Something came up and we won't be able to shoot Olivia's kill tonight."

Everyone erupts into angry mutterings and then Kristen steps closer, looking like she might throw a punch. "Why not?"

Donovan stands his ground, refusing to be intimidated. "There's just been a few changes to the shooting schedule. We'll kill Olivia on Tuesday."

Everyone erupts in annoyed surprise and Warner huffs like an angry locomotive. "How unprofessional to change the shooting schedule at the last moment. I came tonight explicitly to watch that scene."

Kristen glares daggers. "For once, I agree with Mr. Harassment. Very unprofessional, Cass."

Warner scowls at Kristen's insult before staggering off, cursing under his breath, while Asher films him.

Cassie notes the unsteady gait and realizes Warner must've drunk a lot more than what was in that little flask he had earlier. She also reminds herself to ask Asher about his constant filming any time Warner is present. Maybe he's just following her earlier directive, but maybe not.

Olivia folds her arms across her chest and tilts her head, offering that entitled look she's perfected. "This sucks. I was looking forward to my Drew Barrymore moment."

Now Kristen turns on her, smirk in full bloom. "And I was *so* looking forward to directing your *Drew Barrymore* moment."

Olivia sticks out her tongue.

"Shooting schedules change," Donovan asserts, determined to remain in control. "It's something we all better get used to if we're gonna go pro."

William peeks out from behind his bangs while still holding the camera. "So, we're done, then?"

Donovan nods. "Yeah. Let's pack everything up."

William strolls away. Diego stares a long moment at Donovan, as though he might say something, but then follows Kristen as she storms back to the house.

Olivia tosses another angry glower at Cassie and Donovan. "I'm outta here." She stalks off toward a BMW coupe parked at the corner.

Baxter shrugs and offers Asher his bag of chips. Asher dips a hand in and pulls out a fistful, following Baxter over to help William bundle up the dolly track.

Only Jaden stays behind. He's holding the mask in one hand and staring at Donovan with an expression that sends shivers up Cassie's spine. His squinting eyes shimmer beneath the streetlights, like those of a rabid wolf.

Donovan stiffens beside her. "Thanks again for your help with the dolly, Jaden. We got some great stuff thanks to you."

Jaden remains frozen in place, like a stone monument. Cassie is sure the hand not holding the mask is clenched into a fist, but all the shadows make it hard to be certain.

"We know you're disappointed about the kill scene, but it'll happen." She keeps her voice as neutral as she can, despite feeling more afraid of him than ever before.

Jaden says nothing.

She glances at Donovan, but he looks just as spooked. He stands tall and faces Jaden straight on. "We could really use your help packing everything up."

Jaden starts forward suddenly, taking large strides. Cassie holds her breath and Donovan flinches, stepping forward to shield her.

Jaden is only a few feet away now.

"Sure, Donovan." He strides past to join William and his crew returning the sections of track to their respective boxes.

Cassie turns to Donovan, fighting to conceal her unease as she offers a sarcastic, "That went well."

She feels the stiffness leave his body as he tosses her a relieved grin.

"Now we wait," she adds, gloom settling over her again as the reason for changing their schedule hits her like a slap to the face.

Donovan loses his grin. "Yeah, for someone to die."

CHAPTER SEVEN
THE KILLER'S RETRIBUTION

T HE OTHERS HAVE ALL LEFT for home and it's just Donovan and Cassie at her kitchen table, papers and storyboards spread out before them. Donovan watches her, but she's fixated on the schedule for tomorrow when she'll be back in the director's chair. He doesn't take nearly as much prep time, but he has such an artistically visual mind that his finished films often resemble his storyboards to a tee.

Cassie, on the other hand, obsesses over every detail when it's her day to direct, frequently reminding him that her work has to be as perfect as she can make it because she's a female and Hollywood is still a male-dominated industry, especially the Director's Guild. Just last week, they had a conversation about this very subject.

"Look, Cass," he'd said during one of their preproduction meetings, "Hollywood loves to crow about their female directors and the media will fall all over you, so you don't need to be so OCD about everything."

"Yes, I do." She gave him one of those long, deep looks that meant she'd thought a lot about this issue. "I'm a female director and there will be people who'll want to see me fall flat on my face because they feel threatened. Plus, if my films fail at the box office, it will be used against me. You and I could name a bunch of male directors who've had bomb after bomb and still get hired for new projects."

He'd offered his best smile, the one he knows she loves. "And you'd get new assignments, too," he'd assured her, keeping his manner soft and soothing. "Everyone knows it's not just the director's fault if a film fails."

"But the director is the one who gets blamed," she went on, her passion evident in the fiery tone of her voice. "And if it's my film that fails, some in the industry, maybe even lots, will say it's because I can't handle it, that directing is a man's job and I should stick to writing."

He'd nodded, conceding that she had a real point. Hollywood behind the scenes doesn't match up with what Hollywood makes visible to the public, so he let the subject drop.

Sitting at the table now and watching her intense focus, he suddenly wonders if this is the same reason Marisol acts so tough and hard doing her job, but was always so sweet and fun-loving when she'd come over for dinner. Whenever Donovan had spent time around her, she couldn't have been nicer. But then, he'd never dealt with her professional side before. He's beginning to understand that—in certain arenas, at least—being male gives him some unspoken advantages over Cassie that he never considered before. He silently vows to not razz her anymore for being such a perfectionist.

Observing her scrutiny of each and every detail for tomorrow's shoot, his mind wanders back to his mother and how meticulous she's always been, both at home and at work. She keeps their home as sanitized as the hospital rooms that house her patients, which might explain why he's so lackadaisical about his own appearance. A silent, nonaggressive rebellion, perhaps. He's never really given it that much thought. Having never known his dad, who died of stomach cancer when Donovan was a baby, he's grown up as the "man" of the house since he wore diapers.

His mom has always been a great provider, but not someone he could talk to about, well, much of anything. Not like Cassie's dad, who's listened to practically every issue he's ever faced since he was six, from his fears of bullies in elementary school to his hoped-for career as a horror film director. His mom has always pushed him to become a nurse, or better yet, a doctor, even though he sucks at both math and science and his brain has always been hard-wired toward the arts.

He can say without a shred of doubt that he loves Cassie's dad as the father he never had. He loves his mother too, of course, just not in the same way. He knows she loves him and wants the best for him. For some reason, though, she's never wanted him to be himself, but rather her preconceived version of himself. She tries to control *who* he should be, *what* he should like, *when* he should date, *whom* he should date, *what* career he should pursue, and on and on. Maybe it's her nursing background, but she wants to micromanage everything and leave nothing to chance.

What she doesn't accept is that when done right, filmmaking is exactly that kind of profession. Preproduction—part of what Cassie is doing right now—requires meticulous planning before the director ever sets foot on the set. Nothing can be left to chance except such vagaries as the weather, but even then a good director obsesses over weather reports before and during every shoot. So in a way, his choice of profession mirrors hers in the detailed nature of how it's done. Donovan has never understood why she only considers *her* career worth pursuing. Will he ever be able to win her over?

He looks up from the shot sheets for his next shooting day, realizing his mind has wandered *way* off course and he has to start over.

"Nothing from Pop yet?"

So engrossed in studying the storyboards, Cassie doesn't respond.

"Uh, Cass?"

His hand on her arm gets her attention and she glances up, looking annoyed at the interruption. "What?"

He feels like she just stabbed him in the heart.

"Sorry, D-Boy." She glances at her phone. "Nothing. Looks like he was right. The killer *is* spying on us."

The hurt slips from his heart, only to be replaced by fear. "Yeah, but how? You think hoodie guy is the killer?"

She pushes aside the storyboards. "He took off when I saw him. That's pretty suspicious."

He nods, and then his phone vibrates, signaling an incoming text. Picking it up from the tabletop, he opens the message and stiffens, his breathing on hold.

That was very bad form changing the shooting schedule, Donovan. It better not happen again. Just to make sure you know I mean business, your annoying mother will meet with an unfortunate accident. Nothing fatal. Yet. But do not change the schedule again. Or else.

Cassie grasps his arm like a vise. "What?"

Hand trembling, he slides the phone over to her and she scans the text.

Color drains from her face, and her hands shake as she types a message into the phone.

He leans over to read:

Who are you?

There's a moment of tense silence as they both stare at the screen. Then the phone vibrates and this text appears:

This phone cannot receive calls or texts.

Donovan snatches back the phone, punching in a number.

"You calling my dad?"

He shakes his head. "My mom. I have to warn her. You call Pop."

She grabs her phone and hurries into the dining room.

"Mom, you have to get out of there," Donovan says into his phone as he starts pacing.

His mother's exasperated voice drifts out of the handset. "What are you talking about, Donovan? My shift isn't even half over."

Donovan stops, his voice rising in pitch. "I just got a text from the guy who's been stabbing people around here. He says he's gonna hurt you. You need to leave now!"

"You're making no sense, sweetheart. It's those dreadful horror films you watch with Cassie. I do wish you'd outgrow them."

"Mom, this isn't a joke and it's not my imagination. It's real. The killer is after you!"

"Why would he be after me?" His mother's voice sounds patronizing, like she's talking to a five-year-old. "It's my understanding he's been killing homeless people."

Cassie re-enters the kitchen and places a comforting arm around his shoulders. Leaning into his ear, she whispers, "Dad's on his way there now."

"Cassie's dad is on his way over. Please don't be alone until he gets there."

His entire body trembles and Cassie pulls him closer.

"I have my rounds to do, honey and it's late. There aren't many staff on duty, but I'll do my best. Now I really have to go. Love you."

The phone goes silent.

"Mom, wait!"

But the connection has ended.

He gazes at Cassie in stunned horror, his heart hammering wildly with fear. "She doesn't believe me. I need to go over there."

He pockets the phone and pulls away from her, but she grabs his hand and squeezes. "Dad said under no circumstances are we to leave the house. He'll pick up your mom and watch over her."

Donovan frowns, feeling nothing but unmitigated panic that something will happen to his mother, something that's his fault!

He pulls Cassie against his trembling chest and buries his face in her hair, relishing the feel of her comforting arms around him. Quiet tears spill from his eyes and dampen her hair, but he knows she won't think him weak for crying.

Oh, Mom, please be all right!

The overhead nightlights cause the shiny tile floor to shimmer with an iridescent blue tint, casting Marjory's pristine uniform in an otherworldly glow. Shaking her head in annoyance, she slips her cell phone back into the pocket of her uniform.

"What am I going to do with that boy?"

Sighing with the weight of a parent believing she's failed her child, Marjory grips the handle of her four-wheeled push cart and starts down the shadowy corridor. On both sides she eyes the shiny wooden doors twenty feet apart from each other, and then glances at her medication-laden cart with multiple clipboards dangling from hooks along its side. All of these rooms house patients, and most of them require medication. For those who don't, she still must look in on them to notate current status in their charts.

She starts toward the first door, the cart wheels squeaking like church mice. The smell of alcohol permeates the air, typical of every hospital she's ever worked in, the scent barely registering in her finely attuned nostrils. Her mind churns with uncertainty over Donovan's phone call, not because she thinks there's any threat to her life, but because he sounded like *he* believes it.

As much as she loves Cassie and feels that, on most levels, she's a good fit for her son, Marjory recognizes that Cassie's fixation on horror movies isn't healthy for Donovan, and she's certain Cassie must be the cause of his anxiety-ridden phone call. Those teachers at school don't help either, filling his head with fantasies of grandeur in Hollywood. How many kids dream of making it big, only to end up waiting tables their entire lives? She doesn't want that for Donovan. If only she could convince him to pursue something more practical.

The squeaking slows to a halt as she stops outside the first door on her right. Without intending to, she turns and glances back at the deserted nurse's station. Of course, no one's there and she almost kicks herself for letting Donovan's call spook her. While the oppressive lack of sound late at night might be off-putting to some nurses who prefer more human interaction during their shifts, Marjory loves the serenity, which is, for her, a major improvement over the hustle and bustle of a day shift. Scanning the first clipboard, she reaches for a small cup containing two pink pills and then quietly pushes her way into the room.

The patient—an elderly woman recovering from hip surgery—sleeps peacefully in her bed, the dim night light casting a feeble glow on her white hair and pasty complexion. Marjory uses the water jug beside the bed to fill a small cup and then leans in to wake the lady.

For her, this is the hardest part of the night shift because most people don't like being awakened from a sound sleep, especially if they might experience a new round of pain the sleep had been masking. But doctors' orders are doctors' orders.

The lady takes a long moment to pull herself from sleep and fully register Marjory's presence, but once she does her face creases into a smile, splitting her wrinkled cheeks into an expression of pleasure.

"Hello Marjory, time for my pills?" Her voice croaks, likely from dryness in the throat.

"Yes, it is, Mrs. Strode. How's the pain, one to ten?"

"I was dreaming it was a ten," the old lady says, "but now that I'm awake it's maybe a five."

Marjory offers her most comforting smile. "Hopefully, these pills will bring it down to a one."

After Mrs. Strode washes down the pills with a healthy dose of water, she hands Marjory the cup.

"Thank you, Marjory. You're a dear."

And then she's gently snoring once again.

Returning to her cart, Marjory smiles to herself, thinking how nice it would be if all her patients were like sweet Mrs. Strode.

Emerging from the room, she disposes of the now-empty cup in a plastic bag dangling from her cart and makes a notation in Mrs. Strode's chart. Fortunately, this floor houses easy-to-manage patients, unlike some other floors on which she's been stationed where no one has a kind word to say about her or anything else.

As she pushes the cart toward the next door, the sharp squeak of the wheels almost makes her jump. The silence must be getting to her, or else it's that intrusive call from Donovan giving her crazy ideas. Forcing such morbid thoughts from her mind, she stops before the next door and repeats the same procedure as before, making sure to remove the correct medicine from the cart.

Once more, she's in and out of the room in no time. Smiling at the ease of her job, she moves on to the third door. The squeaking eases to a stop and she reaches for the third clipboard. A scuffling sound from behind causes her to whirl around in surprise. The blue-tinted corridor is empty. The nurse's station at the far end looks forlorn and lonely. Shadows stretch across the burnished floor like grasping hands.

But nothing moves.

"Damn you, Donovan," she mutters, shaking off the shiver creeping up her back.

Determined not to let irrational fear get the better of her, she presses on toward the fourth door, stopping to examine the chart. This patient doesn't require medication, just a recording of his vital signs from the monitors. Lifting the clipboard off its hook, she pushes open the thick wooden door and enters the darkened room.

Emerging moments later, she glances up and down the corridor, silently cursing her skittishness as she replaces the now-updated patient chart on its hook. She grips the push handle of her cart, easing it forward. She glances down at the noisy wheels, noting how the polished floor reflects back a blurred rolling image that's almost mesmerizing.

Arriving at the next room on her route, Marjory suddenly feels the chill of the corridor that normally never bothers her. Hospitals are typically cold to keep germ spread to a minimum and she always wears a warm sweater beneath her uniform to ward it off.

So why am I shivering?

Once more allowing her studied gaze to take in the corridor ahead of her, she glances back the way she came.

Empty.

Of course, it is!

She knows she's alone, but can't shake the irrational feeling that she's being watched. It's Donovan and that panicky phone call again! Just the overactive imagination of an immature teenage boy and nothing more than that.

So, why can't she control the rapid beating of her heart and the cold seeping into her bones like melting ice?

Determined to focus on her tasks for the night, she glances at the next room number and then grabs the appropriate clipboard, studying the instructions. This one needs meds, she notes, but the liquid variety injected into his I.V. She studies the various items on her chart, reaching for the syringe labeled with the patient's name and room number. Glancing around once more to assure herself that she is indeed alone, Marjory steps into the room.

The interior is dim, but not completely dark. As in the other rooms, soft illumination from night lights along the off-white walls allow her to see without having to turn on overheads that might wake the patient. She steps to the IV bag and uncaps the syringe, noting that the man in the bed is snoring softly, his head turned away from her and his face in shadow.

He must've been admitted today, she thinks as she prepares the syringe, *because I don't recognize the name.*

Injecting the medicine, she recaps the empty syringe and pockets it before notating on the room chart the time she administered the medication.

She glances once more at the sleeping patient and then returns to the door. Gripping the metal handle, she pulls it inward and steps out into the corridor.

Strong hands seize her around the neck from behind and wrench her brutally backward into the room. Before she can even utter a strangled cry, an explosion of pain fills her head and everything goes black.

Cassie watches Donovan pace her kitchen like a caged animal, his soft features ravaged with fear, his cell phone clutched so tightly in his right hand she fears it will be crushed. She glances at her phone screen—eleven-thirty. And no word from her dad.

She wants to comfort him, but doesn't know how, and that bothers her. Ordinarily, she doesn't lament her less-than-stellar nurturing ability because Donovan more than makes up for her lack and they're so seldom apart. Just observing his dealings with others on a daily basis models for her what she feels should be intrinsic in herself. Her dad is the most understanding person she knows other than Donovan, so she doesn't think her reserved nature is a result of her mother dying when she was so young.

It must just be me, she concludes, *how I am.*

She's always prided herself on being cool and collected and unemotional because those qualities are needed, in her mind, for her chosen profession. But there are times, like now, that require a more empathetic touch, something she needs to improve if she's ever to be that one special person in Donovan's life.

The doorbell chimes, sounding like a bomb in the thick silence of the house. Donovan freezes and Cassie, startled out of her reverie, meets his wide-eyed gaze.

"It might be Marisol," she offers, hesitantly. "Dad said he was gonna call her."

He darts past her. "Let's see."

She leaps from her chair, scraping it against the tile floor, and hurries after him.

Donovan arrives at the front door before her, but waits until she's beside him.

Giving him a cautious look, she leans into the door. "Who's there?"

"It's Detective Santiago, Cassie," comes the muffled reply on the other side of the thick, mahogany door. "Your dad called me."

Donovan flinches.

Cassie presses her eye to the peephole before unlocking the deadbolt and swinging open the door. Dressed in her typical-style pantsuit and low heels, with not a hair out of place, Marisol steps inside. Cassie glances out at the dark street a moment before closing and locking the door.

Donovan stands rigid, like he's been turned to stone. "Why are you here, Marisol? Did something happen to my mom?" His voice sounds like a spring that's wound tight enough to snap.

Marisol wears a grim expression on her attractive face. "Let's talk in the living room."

She exits the foyer and heads down the hall, her heels clicking ominously against the hardwood floor.

Tears blur Donovan's hazel eyes as Cassie grabs him awkwardly by the arm and leads him after Marisol.

Donovan has his hands wrapped around his face as Marisol shares the news of the attack on his mom. Her heart pounding, Cassie sweeps an arm across his shoulders and pulls his head against her, once more at a loss for words.

"I should've gone right over there," he mumbles between lurching gulps for air.

"You'd have been too late," Marisol assures him in a soothing voice.

He pulls his tear-streaked face away from Cassie like a turtle emerging from its shell. "How do you know that?"

"From what Officer Stewart said, she was attacked shortly after your phone conversation."

Cassie gazes at her intently, keeping her voice steady for Donovan's sake. "But she'll be all right. That's what you said."

Marisol nods. "Yes. She has a concussion from the blow to her head and will need to be hospitalized for several days, but she should be fine. I've stationed an officer outside her room twenty-four seven until this maniac is caught."

Cassie takes that information at face value, hoping Marisol isn't just spinning for Donovan's sake. She decides to focus on the attacker.

"Can you trace the phone number?"

Marisol looks dubious. "Doubtful. It's likely a burner phone, the kind drug dealers use to hide their tracks, and probably at the bottom of the ocean by now."

Cassie keeps a tight hold on Donovan. He's stopped crying, but the tightness of his body and the tremors rumbling through him broadcast his grief like a loudspeaker.

"So, what now?" She gazes at Marisol with raised eyebrows. "If we stop filming, Donovan's—uh, someone could get hurt or... worse."

"Yes. The killer clearly wants you to finish this film. But if you do keep filming, the murders are likely to continue."

"He also knows our shooting schedule," Cassie adds as the thought slips into her mind.

"I'd say that's a safe bet. But he's spying on the actual shooting or he wouldn't have known you moved that kill scene. You've been using a drone?"

"Yeah, why?" Cassie fights an irrational fear that Marisol might cite them for using the drone. But then she remembers that her dad got clearance from the police department.

Marisol studies her with an expression that's all-business, so different from the affectionate surrogate mom who used to come over for dinner almost every night.

"I'll want to see all that footage ASAP. It's possible the drone camera captured the killer lurking off to the sidelines without you knowing it."

The idea of someone watching their every move unnerves Cassie. "Okay. I can put it all on a flash drive for you."

"What night will you film that kill scene?"

"Tuesday, since Donovan's directing it." She glances down at him, but his glazed eyes stare across the room without any indication he heard his name. "We alternate days." Another thought strikes her. "What about Robert? Will he be released?"

"Not yet."

Thoughts and images churn through Cassie's head as she pictures Robert.

"Do you know which hand the killer held the knife in, you know, when he pinned that guy to the tree?"

Marisol hesitates a moment, as though mulling over the spilling of state secrets. "His right."

Cassie feels momentarily excited. "Robert's left-handed."

"I know. I watched him sign his statement. But he could still be an accomplice."

Cassie deflates. "Yeah, that's true."

"All I can do right now is pore through your drone footage and have officers stationed in a perimeter around your locations over the next few days. I'll also need the full script and shooting schedule. Are you killing anyone tomorrow?"

"No. Just dialogue stuff in the afternoon and stalking scenes after dark."

Marisol's face takes on a look of resolve. "So Tuesday's our focus. I'll have officers patrolling a three-mile radius around your location. Hopefully, we can catch this guy before anyone else is killed."

"Should I tell the cast and crew what's going on?"

"Negative. With Robert possibly involved, there could be others. All they need to know if they comment on the police presence is that your dad was worried over the murders and requested extra officers in the area."

Cassie's heartrate leaps into hyperdrive and she glances at Donovan.

He looks up at Marisol, a shocked look on his face. "Do you really think someone from the film is the killer?"

Marisol eyes him with the hopelessness that clearly comes from witnessing too much evil out on the streets.

"Donovan, in my experience, anything is possible."

Donovan locks eyes with Cassie and she senses his fear as clearly as if it were her own.

"That drone footage, Cass?" Marisol glances at her watch. "We're pressed for time here."

Cassie pulls her mind back into focus. "Oh, right."

She releases Donovan and jumps up from the couch, hurrying from the room.

Donovan wipes residual tears from his eyes. Marisol places a surprisingly gentle hand on his shoulder.

"There was really nothing you could've done, Donovan. We'll protect your mother, don't worry."

He studies her resolute face for a long moment, but doesn't respond.

CHAPTER EIGHT

A SHOCKING REVELATION

ONOVAN TOSSES AND TURNS THROUGHOUT night, beset by images of his mother attacked and brutally murdered before his eyes while he remains frozen in place. He wakes up five different times, soaked in sweat and trembling with terror. Finally, at five o'clock, he gives up on the idea of sleep and staggers into the shower, where warm water washes away the clammy dampness coating his body like slime, but does nothing to wash away his guilt.

After throwing on whatever pieces of his clothing still hang in the hall closet, he lumbers down the long hallway to the kitchen and does something he's never done before—starts the coffee maker for *himself*. As dark-colored water percolates into the round glass container, Donovan plops heavily into a chair at the dinette table and lays his head down on the soft placemat.

Sometime later, he is jolted upright by a loud *beep beep beep* and realizes he must've dozed off. Glancing around the kitchen as morning light filters through the lace curtains he helped Cassie pick out, he realizes the beeping comes from the coffee maker signaling the completion of its cycle. He rises and sets the device to "warm" mode before pouring himself a cup.

By the time Edward enters the kitchen, Donovan is back at the table sipping the hot coffee from a mug emblazoned with a slashing knife and the words "Halloween 40th Anniversary." They make brief eye contact as Edward pulls his mug from the cupboard and fills it to the brim before moving to the table. He must've come home while Donovan was in the shower, because he's not in uniform but, rather, dressed in jeans and a long-sleeve pullover shirt. He takes a long sip from his mug that says 'Dad is King' in thick gold letters.

"I thought you hated coffee."

Donovan looks up. "I do. But I hardly slept and it'll keep me awake."

"Son, your mom will be fine."

"What if he comes after her again?"

"She's under constant guard, and it isn't your fault someone decided to copycat your film."

Donovan feels nauseous with remorse. "If I wasn't making a horror movie in the first place, my mom would be okay."

Edward sets down his mug and places both arms on the table, leaning forward. "Donovan, listen to me. There are nuts out there who could turn a romcom into an excuse for killing."

"Yeah, but movies like ours give them ideas."

"Son, real evil is far worse than anything a nice kid like you could dream up. Psychos don't need movies to copy, but sometimes they get off on it. Stop beating yourself up and finish this film. That's the only way we can catch this guy."

Donovan meets Edward's intense gaze and his heart swells with understanding.

Cassie ambles in dressed in slacks and a blue tee shirt, bushy hair pinned back off her face. She eyes them both curiously.

"Everything all right?"

Edward nods. "Yeah. Just a father reminding his son that he's a good kid."

Cassie knits her brow, looking from one to the other in confusion. Donovan offers a tiny smile of assurance, and she relaxes.

"What's your schedule today?"

Hearing Edward's question, Cassie pulls her gaze from Donovan to meet her dad's eyes. "We start filming at noon over at William's place."

"I'll be back on duty at dusk, but I might swing by before then to search the area, see if I can spot anyone watching the shoot."

"Thanks, Dad." She turns to Donovan. "You ready to go over the shot sheets with me?"

Donovan purposely offers her that little smile he knows she loves and follows her from the kitchen, leaving a concerned Edward sipping his coffee in silence.

Donovan hates everything about hospitals, from the smells to the starkness of the décor to the very sight of sick people, which is why he almost never visits his mother at work. When he was younger and she'd drag him along for "Bring Your Child To Work Day," he'd close his eyes most of the time, counting the minutes until he could go home. Even school was better than the hospital! Every time he reminds his mother of his hospital phobia as the best reason he could never become a doctor or nurse, her response is the same as it is about horror films: "You'll outgrow it."

Today, he sits in a stiff plastic chair inside a sterile-looking room gazing at his mother, not in her role as a nurse, but in a role she's never played before—a patient tucked carefully beneath the covers of a hospital bed. The tightly wrapped bandages covering the entire top of her head look like a turban and there are several beeping machines recording her vital signs. There's also an IV dripping some clear liquid through a thin tube into a needle taped to her forearm. He knows from her teachings that the liquid is likely saline, or maybe glucose to provide nutrients for when she's not up to eating solid food.

His chest clenches like a fist and, despite what Cassie's dad said earlier this morning, remorse floods his heart and soul. Her eyes flutter open again. That's a good sign; the doctors and nurses assured him of that when he'd arrived an hour ago. And even though she's been drifting in and out of sleep, she sounds lucid when she speaks.

"Can I get you anything, Mom? Are you comfortable?"

She shifts her gaze sideways and squints at him. "My head feels like it's been split open."

Another stab to Donovan's heart. "I'm so sorry, Mom." He pauses, considering how best to say what's on his mind. "I... I been thinking about this all morning. I'm gonna quit the film and stay here until you come home. You're more important."

Her eyebrows arch in surprise. "You'd do that for me?"

He nods. The last thing he wants is to quit the film, but it's *because* of the film that she's in this bed in the first place, recovering from a serious blow to the head that could easily have killed her.

She offers a gentle smile. "Thank you, son. I know I've been hard on you about your career choice, but Edward reminded me again last night that I have to let you grow up. And I do, don't I?"

Confused, Donovan leans in closer. "What are you saying, Mom?"

"You need to finish what you started, honey. Isn't that what I've always taught you?"

Donovan squints at her, his mind whirling in bewilderment. "But you hate what I do."

She smiles again, looking beautiful despite the head bandage. "I don't need to love what you do to love *you*, do I?"

Warmth fills his insides. "I… I love you, Mom."

Her eyelids flutter with exhaustion. "Back at you." She drifts off to sleep.

Feeling closer to his mother than ever before, Donovan leans in to kiss her gently on the cheek before leaving the room, his step much lighter than when he entered. He nods to the officer sitting outside the door, relieved that the man looks like an NFL linebacker who could toss grown men around with ease.

"Thanks for watching over my mom," he says, genuinely grateful.

The cop, whose name tag reads "Riley" (ironic because that's the name of the deputy sheriff in *Scream*), tips his blue cap. "My pleasure, kid."

Buoyed with renewed hope, Donovan leaves the hospital and heads back to the shoot.

William's house has always been one of Cassie's favorites. It's one of the few three-story homes she's ever seen and his small, shuttered third floor window always screams *Psycho* house to her horror film sensibilities, making the place a perfect backdrop. It doesn't look anything like the real *Psycho* house, of course, but its Craftsman style architecture is gorgeous. A covered front porch, deeply overhanging roof eaves, single dormers for each floor, and tapered columns supporting the roof are all old-school enough that, at night and with the right lighting, the house looks haunted.

William utters a quiet, "Earth to Cassie."

She turns to him with a smile, losing it quickly when she spots Olivia flirting with Diego near the front door, and Kristen a short distance away glaring daggers at them both.

"Here we go again," William adds, indicating the trio, his tone one of exasperation.

Cassie nods as a red Ford Escape sporting a sticker proclaiming "I Teach. What's Your Superpower?" affixed to the rear bumper pulls up to the curb. The Ketchum's exit and amble over to join the group.

Cassie crosses the lawn to meet them, Donovan jogging over to join her. "Mr. and Mrs. Ketchum. We didn't expect you. Everything all right?"

Mr. Ketchum has a troubled, drawn look etched across his features. "With your film, yes, Cassie. But these murders…." He trails off, scanning the cast and crew staring at him in surprise. "You know I don't hover when my students are filming, but I'm quite concerned about this."

Mrs. Ketchum slips an arm through his and pulls him close. "A Detective Santiago dropped by the morning and shared some disturbing information, so we decided to check for ourselves how things are going."

A wave of guilt washes over Mr. K's face. "Donovan, I'm so sorry about your mother. The detective told us."

Donovan nods, his face blooming with color.

"We'd visit her in the hospital," Mrs. K says to break the awkward moment, "but given her antipathy toward us…" She trails off awkwardly.

Donovan finds his voice. "It's okay."

Mr. K's gaze skims over Cassie and the others. "I confess I was tempted to pull the plug on this film when the detective told us the killer is copying you."

Cassie flinches like she's been shot. "But—"

"I talked him out of it, Cass," Mrs. K interjects before Cassie can go on. "And Detective Santiago was against that idea, too, though she didn't say why."

"She assured me there would be plenty of police presence," Mr. K adds, still looking indecisive and shifting from foot to foot.

Mrs. K pulls him closer. "We did pass three police cruisers on our way over here, darling." She offers him a reassuring look.

He studies the kids. "Still, you're my responsibility, not the detective's."

Donovan takes a step forward. "Mr. K, we're being super careful and Cass's dad cruises by, like, every fifteen minutes."

The Ketchum's exchange a thoughtful look, but before the conversation can continue, Mr. Warner saunters up the sidewalk in their direction, wearing his black porkpie hat and a loud Hawaiian-style shirt.

"Well, well, what brings you out here, Randy?" He tips his hat to Mrs. K. "Connie."

She offers a gracious smile, but says nothing.

Mr. K studies Warner a long moment. "Just checking on my kids. You behaving yourself, Ron?"

Kristen storms over, followed closely by Diego and Olivia. "No, he's not, Mr. K. He's still leering at us every chance he gets."

Diego looks happy to see their teacher and offers a wide smile. "How's it going, Mr. K?"

"I'm worried, Diego." He glares at Warner. "Ron, I thought Cassie laid it out for you with great clarity. Either you get your career back on track or become on internet poster boy for harassment."

Mrs. K flushes with obvious embarrassment. "Randy, that's no way to treat your old friend." She offers Warner an apologetic look.

Mr. K keeps his gaze pinned to Warner. "Acquaintance, not friend. And if I get any more reports from these girls about your behavior, Ron, I'll personally upload those videos they shot."

Warner huffs indignantly, but Cassie has the odd sensation that he's feigning offense, rather than feeling it. He glowers at Mr. K. "You always were a bore, even as a drunk."

He tips his hat once again to Mrs. K, who wears an expression of deep mortification, and saunters off down the street.

"Jerk," Olivia mutters after him.

Mr. K glances around at the kids with sincere regret. "I'm sorry, Cass and Donovan, and all of you, for bringing him on board. I thought having a name actor, besides my wife, of course, might get your film more attention."

Cassie shrugs. "It's not your fault, Mr. K."

Donovan adds quickly, "He's only got one shooting day left, anyway."

"The warehouse?" Mr. K glances from one to the other.

They nod simultaneously.

"Ah yes, the warehouse," Mrs. K repeats, casting a sideways glance at her husband. "I never read those pages."

"You can read them now," Cassie assures her, smiling. "I just didn't want the other cast members to see them."

"We'll come watch the night shoot," Mr. K assures them, his tone thick with tension, "because I'll be too stressed to sit at home."

Her arm wrapped within his, Mrs. K adds, "We'd be devastated if any of you got hurt."

"Thanks," Cassie replies, feeling a sense of warmth trickle through her. Mrs. K has mothered all of them these past four years.

An awkward silence falls over the group until Donovan clears his throat. "Uh, Cass, we're behind schedule."

"Right." She smiles at the Ketchum's. "Excuse us."

They nod, and she waves her cast and crew toward the house.

"Okay, everyone, we're going for the first take. Places, please."

She glances back to note the Ketchum's strolling back to their car before turning her focus to the task at hand.

Marisol sits at her impeccably neat desk within the LAPD Detective Bureau in downtown Los Angeles, concentrating on her flat screen computer monitor. She's vaguely aware of her pale blue nail polish flashing under the office lights as she deftly manipulates the mouse across a pad emblazoned with the LAPD logo. Images dance across her screen, aerial shots of Cassie, Donovan, and their crew scrolling past as she checks each location for anything that looks amiss.

She squints a moment at an area across the street from Cassie and crew, but the offending smudge turns out to be, on closer inspection, a mailbox. The scenes drift past her field of vision, each one similar to the ones she's already viewed, but she examines every sequence with the practiced eye of a detail-oriented detective.

She freezes, her hand on the mouse rigid, and narrows her eyes to study the suspicious image she's spotted on her screen. Forcing herself to move, she clicks on a large tree adjacent to the shooting location she's scrutinizing. She slides the mouse to zoom in on the tree.

Closer and closer.

She bends forward as a figure, wearing what looks like a gray hoodie, comes into focus. But the image is still too pixelated to make out the face. Marisol taps the keyboard, grateful for the department's image-enhancing software, and the figure gradually becomes clearer. The face is almost visible…

She leans in so close she could almost kiss the screen. "It can't be…"

Pulling away, she sits back in her office chair, ignoring the squeak as it tilts. Frowning in disbelief, she gazes intently at the monitor before grabbing for the desk phone and punching in a number.

The only actors on-call for the night scenes are Kristen, Diego, and Jaden, but Donovan knows that doesn't mean they're free of any more Olivia drama. She's still inside William's house removing her makeup.

The dolly tracks have been laid out in the street parallel to the tree-lined sidewalk. Because of the cracked asphalt, it had taken them well over an hour to get everything in place so the dolly rolls smoothly without any creaking of the wheels. Axle grease comes in handy on occasion.

Baxter stands beside the dolly cleaning his glasses with his tee shirt hem, while William affixes the tripod to the dolly platform, locking it into place and tightening the bolts. As Baxter replaces his glasses and retrieves his spider-like drone from the pavement at his feet, Cassie points out certain angles, and then he releases the drone. It zips high above them, and he munches some chips from yet another bag in his fanny pack as he fingers the remote, sending the "insect" diving and swooping down and around the front yard.

Donovan, wearing a purple fedora, baggy long-sleeve button down shirt and corduroy slacks, stands off to one side, scanning the area as Diego saunters over. Diego's costume consists of cargo pants and a tight long-sleeve pullover shirt that accentuates his chiseled physique.

"Hey, Donovan, what's up with him?" He points to the dark, unmoving form of Jaden. Silhouetted against a pool of light from a streetlamp overhead, he looks like the shadowy, murderous psychopath from every horror flick ever made.

Donovan pulls his gaze from Jaden and faces Diego, who's backlit by one of their portable lights and looks just as menacing as Jaden. "I don't know. He's always been kind of—"

"Weird?" Diego suggests, cutting him off.

"Shy," Donovan finishes, searching for Diego's light brown eyes in the gloom. "But since we started filming, he's been acting…" This time, he trails off, searching for the right word.

"Weird?" Diego offers, with what looks like a smile.

Donovan sighs. "Yeah."

Diego glances past Donovan toward Jaden. "I tried talking to him at lunch, but he blew me off."

"That's cause you let Kristen bully him."

"Like I could stop Lady Macbeth?"

"Good point."

"I think he's crushing on Cass." Diego glances at Cassie, now conversing with William beside the dolly.

"That's what I think, too," Donovan says, feeling a sense of camaraderie with Diego he never has before, "but she isn't so sure. Anyway, are you and Kristen ready to shoot?"

"Yeah."

Cassie calls out, "Actors, take your places. We're going for a take."

Diego smiles at Donovan. "And there's my cue." He gazes a moment longer, his intensity almost making Donovan squirm, and then strikes out across the grass toward Cassie and William.

Wondering what that final look was all about, Donovan joins the group gathered around Cassie.

"We'll shoot the master and reverse and then do closeups," she says, casting her gaze from face to face.

"As usual," Kristen sneers. "We know the drill, Cassie."

When Cassie glowers, Kristen turns to Diego. "What did I say?"

He tilts his head and purses his full lips before tossing Donovan a glance that screams *see what I mean*, clearly referencing their earlier conversation.

"Places, everyone," Cassie intones in her most serious voice, obviously deciding to ignore Kristen's standard impertinence.

Kristen, dressed in a stylish top and designer jeans that hug every inch of her hips, a large shoulder bag draped over her left side, steps onto her mark in front of the dolly. William stands atop the wooden platform just behind the camera while Donovan places himself at the rear. He's pushing the dolly tonight, since Jaden is in killer mode.

Diego jogs off down the street and awaits his cue. Jaden, silent as a cat, takes up his position behind a thick-trunked Ficus tree, one of many lining this residential street. Its heavy branches—which look like separate trunks unto themselves—and the dense foliage drooping down from above, make this tree the perfect hiding place.

Cassie hurries to the video monitor on William's front lawn and takes her seat in the folding chair, large headphones over her hears.

"Roll camera!"

"Camera rolling," William calls back, and a moment later adds, "Speed."

"Action!"

Kristen, in full nice-girl-Ashley mode, strolls alongside the sidewalk, away from the camera, lost in thought, clearly in no hurry. Donovan eases the dolly forward, pressing his feet hard to the ground and wincing at the pain in his calves. They've rehearsed this scene twice already and his calf muscles are already throbbing.

He's amazed by how easily Jaden handled this thing!

As "Ashley" passes the first thick Ficus trunk, Jaden, in the killer mask, peers out, large knife gripped in one hand. "Ashley" moves farther up the street, and he darts out from behind the tree. Keeping to the sidewalk, he stalks her. The camera follows.

"Ashley" continues her casual walk, her fancy sneakers making the barest of footfalls against the pavement. She stops suddenly, and the camera stops too. Jaden ducks behind another thick tree trunk as she turns and looks back the way she came.

"Hello?" Her voice sounds tense and tight, like an overly wound spring. "Is someone there?"

She awaits a response, but nothing moves. The breeze rustles her long blonde hair and she pushes it away from her face, as though fearing it will block her vision. When nothing moves, she turns and continues walking, but faster this time, like she might break into a frantic run at any moment.

The "killer" slithers around the tree trunk and watches her move away before slinking after her, knife raised to strike. Donovan, sweat beading his forehead as he struggles from the exertion, makes sure the dolly is right behind him so William can keep them both in the frame.

"Ashley" stops with a suddenness that nearly catches Donovan off-guard. He pulls hard on the handles and digs in his feet just as the "killer" ducks behind another tree and "Ashley" calls out in a meek voice, "I know someone's there. I… I have pepper spray."

Keeping her gaze fixed on the dark street behind her, she slips a small spray can from her shoulder bag and holds it up, her arm shaking with fear. Still, nothing moves or makes a sound. She studies the tree behind which the "killer" lurks but, satisfied no one is there, turns and hurries more rapidly up the street, almost jogging.

Donovan digs in and pushes the dolly faster, blinking away the sweat dripping into his eyes and fighting to ignore the burning pain in his calves and shoulders.

Once again, the "killer" sprints after "Ashley," knife raised for the kill. He manages to muffle his footfalls by running atop the adjacent grass. Just as he narrows the gap, a figure leaps from behind a tree in front of "Ashley" and, arms raised, screams in her face, "Aaaahhhh!"

The "killer" lurches back behind a thick tree trunk as "Ashley" skids to a terrified halt, raises the pepper spray and depresses the plunger, apparently squirting liquid into the newcomer's face.

The figure screams in pain and clamps both hands over his face. The sound of his voice causes "Ashley" to freeze and lower the can in surprise.

"Pedro!" she cries as he twists and turns in agony. "What the hell are you doing?"

Diego, playing her boyfriend "Pedro," lowers his hands, but his face remains scrunched up in pain. "Just messing with you. Damn, Ash, what's with the spray?"

She slips the can back into her bag and leans closer to see his face. "There's a killer around here, remember? Oh, hell, let's get you inside."

She leads him toward William's house, as it becomes obvious he cannot see clearly.

From his position behind the tree, the killer watches them retreat.

"Cut!" Cassie's voice pounds though the night like a sonic boom and she leaps to her feet, slipping off the headphones. "That looked awesome!

It's a great master shot. Terrific acting, especially you, Diego. I thought she really sprayed you."

Diego grins broadly and bows, glancing over at Donovan.

"I agree," Donovan says, walking over and forcing himself not to wince from the pain in his calves. Diego is in much better shape and Donovan doesn't want to look like the wimp everyone thinks he is. Cassie doesn't care that he's not athletic, which is all that matters, but he's not in the mood for snarky comments from Kristen.

Squealing in delight, Olivia rushes out the front door and throws her arms around Diego like she hasn't seen him in ages.

"You were amazing!"

Her manufactured gushing is one of the worst cases of overacting Donovan has ever seen, but it apparently works because Kristen's blue eyes flash with stormy anger and she rushes over, snatching Diego by the hand and yanking him away from Olivia's clutches like the other girl has rabies. Kristen's lovely face twists into murderous rage as she drags him toward the large tree.

"I'm gonna kill her one of these days, for real!"

Diego looks shocked at Kristen's vitriol and winces from the pain of her vise-like grip on his forearm.

Olivia smirks gleefully and ambles over to join Cassie, whose frown displays her distaste.

"Olivia, enough with the personal drama. We have a film to finish."

Olivia casts a dreamy expression in Diego's direction. "He's just so hot."

Cassie sighs.

"I'm outta here. Later, people." Olivia struts away toward her Beemer across the street.

Donovan watches her go, to make sure she enters her car safely. Once her lights and engine have engaged, he's satisfied and turns to watch Diego attempting to calm Kristen, who viciously pantomimes choking someone.

Cassie taps him on the shoulder and points.

Donovan turns to see Jaden loitering near the sidewalk, wearing the mask and gripping the handle of his knife like it's a talisman.

"I think we should finish as soon as possible," he says, glancing from the lurking Jaden to the fuming Kristen, "before the cast loses it completely."

She announces, "Okay, everybody, back to one."

Another master, the reverse, and numerous closeups later, Cassie feels good about the footage they've shot. William's camerawork and lighting are perfect for the mood of dread she's aiming for and she can't wait to get into the editing room and stitch this film together. She loves directing more than editing, but having drama queens like Olivia and Kristen on set can make that part of the process quite trying.

She glances over at her dad, in full uniform beside his police cruiser chatting with Mr. and Mrs. K. They all showed up about thirty minutes ago, standing guard as promised. Ordinarily, she would feel uncomfortable having Mr. K watch her at work, but not this time. Tonight, she welcomes the presence of the most important adults in her life.

Edward focuses on his conversation with the Ketchum's, but his eyes skim the street behind them for anything amiss.

"I'm very proud of Cassie and Donovan," Mr. Ketchum is saying, drawing Edward's eyes back to those of the film teacher. "They're great kids."

Edward smiles, glancing over to where Cassie and Donovan supervise the packing of equipment into his SUV.

"I'd like to take some of the credit for that, but they're just great on their own."

Mrs. Ketchum studies the kids. She sports hip-hugging jeans, wavy hair worn shoulder length, and just enough make-up to highlight her cheekbones and accentuate her green eyes.

"They make a cute couple, too," she says, tossing Edward a knowing smile.

"They do, but Cassie insists on no romance until she gets started in her career. Donovan seems okay with it, too, staying friends for now. Works for me either way. I love 'em both."

Mrs. Ketchum nods. "This is your most talented class in years, Randy. They're going places." Her smile droops. "Except maybe that one." She indicates Jaden, standing off by himself holding the skull mask in one hand. "Too standoffish. He's not right in the head."

"You've met his parents, Connie," Mr. Ketchum says, his tone chastising. "The apple doesn't fall far from the tree."

She offers a conciliatory nod. "That's true."

Cassie and Donovan trot over, grinning.

"Well, we're almost wrapped for the night," Cassie informs them, clearly unable to hide her excitement. "No problems to report."

"That's what I like to hear," Mr. Ketchum says, sounding relieved.

The sound of cars draws everyone's attention to a police cruiser, followed by an unmarked sedan, pulling up the street and easing to a stop behind Edward's black and white. Two officers exit the cruiser and Marisol steps from the sedan, looking attractive, Edward can't help but note, in her navy-blue business skirt and matching jacket over a white blouse.

"Checking on the shoot, Detective?" Edward indicates the kids. "They're all done for the night."

Cassie asked hopefully, "Anything new on the case?"

"Unfortunately, yes."

Marisol waves the two officers forward. Edward knows them from the precinct—Dennings and Dyer. They step behind Mr. Ketchum.

"Hands behind your back, sir," Dyer intones, holding out some handcuffs.

Mr. K looks startled, while Cassie gasps and Edward flinches.

Mrs. K stares open-mouthed at Dyer. "Is this some kind of sick joke?"

"Do as he says," Marisol orders, looking hard at Mr. Ketchum.

Baffled, Mr. Ketchum slips his hands behind his back and Dyer snaps on the cuffs. The *click* sound breaks the quiet night air with a terrifying note of finality.

"What's the meaning of this?" Mr. Ketchum gazes at Marisol, outrage filling his wide eyes.

Edward steps forward to confront Marisol. "What the hell's this about, Mari—Detective?"

Marisol ignores him, keeping her gaze fixed on Ketchum. "Mr. Ketchum, you're under arrest for the murder of Mr. Blair, the victim on the park bench."

Mr. Ketchum's face collapses in shock. "You must be joking."

Cassie lurches forward. "That's crazy, Marisol. Mr. K couldn't kill anyone."

Marisol ignores the interruption, focusing on Dyer and Dennings. "Mirandize him and then take him downtown for questioning. I'll follow."

"Yes, Detective." Dyer grabs Mr. Ketchum by one arm and leads him toward the black and white. Dennings follows.

Mrs. Ketchum leaps out in front of Dyer, arms outstretched like a referee. "This is insane! My husband had nothing to do with those murders."

Marisol joins her officers. "Step aside, please, ma'am. He'll have a chance to present his case."

Mrs. Ketchum throws her arms around her husband and wrenches him into a bone-crushing hug. "I'll get Chris on the phone right away. He'll know a good criminal lawyer. Don't say anything till one gets there."

Face devoid of color and looking as though he might faint, Mr. K nods robotically before being led away to the squad car. Dennings pops open the rear door and Dyer assists Mr. Ketchum into the back seat.

His wife gapes in unabashed horror as both cops enter the car, then turns to Edward. "I have to get hold of our attorney. Excuse me."

As she sprints toward her car, Edward turns his angry glare on Marisol. "The hell, Marisol! In front of the kids? He's their teacher, not some random thug!"

Marisol's hard expression melts slightly as she glances at the horrified Cassie and Donovan.

"His fingerprints were found on the murder weapon. And he's the guy in the gray hoodie who's been skulking around. I spotted him in the drone footage."

Donovan's face takes on a look of intense resolve. "Mr. K is the nicest, coolest teacher I've ever had."

"He never even loses his temper," Cassie adds, earning a hearty nod from Donovan.

"That's what people say about every serial killer."

Edward surges with anger. "Marisol!"

She gazes at him and softens again. She leans in toward him, but both kids move closer too. "First Robert, then the teacher. I know it doesn't add up. We're being played."

"I agree," Edward says. "The real killer is still out there."

"Which is why every available cop will be out in force tomorrow night when the kids film that kill scene. But I can't ignore hard evidence, Officer Stewart. You know that. Between us, I'm hoping Ketchum has a solid alibi."

"If he doesn't?" Donovan asks.

She eyes him a long moment, but doesn't answer his question. "I have to get downtown. I'll see you tomorrow night. Be ready for anything."

Without a backward glance, she hurries to her sedan. In seconds, she's off down the street, following the squad car with Mr. Ketchum inside.

"Oh, Dad." Cassie throws her arms around Edward and grips him tightly.

"He's innocent, Cass. Somebody's messing with us, like Detective Santiago said."

"What's he doing here?"

Edward turns in the direction Donovan is indicating.

Warner stands just up the street in the shadows wearing his porkpie hat and topcoat.

"Again?" Edward eyes Donovan with raised eyebrows.

Cassie releases her dad. "Yeah. He keeps hanging around even when he's not on call. Creeps me out big time."

As though knowing he's being talked about, Warner tips his hat and wanders off in the opposite direction.

"I'm gonna do some checking on him," Edward says, returning his gaze to Cassie.

She exchanges a quick look with Donovan before asking, "What will we tell the others about Mr. K?"

Her dad considers a moment. "These kids here saw what happened, so tell *them* the truth, but not the others, at least not until after the kill scene tomorrow night. Is it true that Jaden kid is a bit off?"

Cassie and Donovan exchange a guarded look.

"Maybe," Donovan says, his voice hesitant. "But I think he's just super shy."

"I'll check out his background. Anyone else I should check out?"

Cassie's eyes go wide.

"What?" Her dad leans in so the watching crew members can't hear.

"Well, he's a really nice kid, and it probably doesn't mean anything, but Asher has been acting kind of strange."

Donovan looks surprised. "Asher?"

She nods. "Every time Warner's on set, I see Asher filming him when Warner's not looking."

Donovan doesn't seem surprised. "I've seen that too, but you told everyone to film him, remember?"

"Yeah, but he's the only one doing it all the time."

Her dad fidgets. "His last name?"

"Doyle."

"Got it. Now let's get you packed up and safely home."

CHAPTER NINE

OLIVIA GETS HER DREW BARRYMORE MOMENT

"**MR.** K is not a killer."

Donovan's soft voice punctures the bubble within Cassie's mind, echoing her thoughts exactly.

"No, he's not."

They sit together at her kitchen table, shot sheets and storyboards spread out around them, cans of soda and a bowl of chips in the center. Donovan sets down the storyboard he's examining and gazes intently into her face from beneath his bright yellow fedora.

Cassie knows she must look as distraught as she feels, because she barely brushed her hair this morning and threw on whatever clothes were close at hand, not paying attention to color or style matches. She hardly slept and feels like a zombie, but offers him a tight smile, grateful as always for his constant presence in her life. She can't imagine what she'd do without him.

When's the last time she told him that? Or has she ever?

The front door opening and closing draws her attention toward the hall door. Her dad enters, unstrapping his thick utility belt.

"Hi, Dad."

He looks dog-tired as he plops down into the nearest chair and lays the heavily laden belt down in an open spot on the table. Cassie eyes the cuffs, pepper spray, taser, and other accoutrements of her dad's profession, always amazed by how much stuff he's required to carry around while on duty. He unclips his baton and lays it beside the belt.

"I'm home for the rest of the day. Back out tonight." He studies Donovan. "What's the word on your mom?"

"She's better today, but they wanna keep her a couple more nights, even though she wants out. She hates being a patient."

Edward nods. "Feisty as ever. That's a good sign."

Cassie leans in expectantly. "Find out anything at the station, Dad?"

Edward's lined face looks sober. "Yeah. But bear in mind, what I'm telling you doesn't leave this room."

Donovan nods and Cassie says, "Absolutely."

"Okay. Mr. Ketchum has priors, that's why his fingerprints were identified so quickly."

Donovan flinches. "Priors for what?"

"DUI, bar fights, drunk and disorderly in public. Spent some time in county. He gets ugly when he drinks."

Donovan frowns. "That doesn't sound like the Mr. K we know."

"You know the sober version," Edward replies, stifling a yawn and slouching forward in his chair like he might fall asleep any moment.

Cassie wants to know more. "What about Warner?"

"Same. The two of 'em got busted together a few times, along with Mrs. Ketchum, by the way. In Warner's case, he was accused of blaming his limo driver for a crash when he was allegedly the one behind the wheel. The driver insisted he was innocent, but did jail time for drunk driving and reckless endangerment. When he got out, he was blackballed by the industry."

"Mrs. K always says there's no such thing as bad publicity." Cassie glances at Donovan and he nods in confirmation.

Edward shrugs. "Doesn't hold true for limo drivers, apparently. The guy killed himself a few years later. Sad story."

"It's tragic," Cassie exclaims, her heart heavy with sorrow. "There was no evidence against Warner?"

"Just his word against the driver's and Warner had the more expensive attorney."

"What'd you find out about Jaden?" Donovan asks, his voice tinged with concern.

Edward's face slides from stoicism to melancholy. "That one's sad too.

I can't go into details even with you, but Jaden's been in and out of foster care over the years. Could explain the shyness everyone reads as 'creepy.'"

"Damn," Donovan mutters. "What about Asher?"

"Model student, from what I was able to glean from his school records," Edward says, his eyelids sagging with fatigue. "His mother had him modeling up through middle school, but that stopped when he entered Performing Arts High. Like you said, Cass, seems like a good kid."

Cassie nods. "I get the whole modeling thing. He's beautiful."

Donovan jerks his head around to stare at her.

She focuses on her dad. "None of this helps Mr. K."

Edward sighs tiredly. "No, Cass, not till after you shoot Olivia's kill tonight. If there's no attempted copycat murder, Ketchum's in serious trouble."

Cassie considers a moment, twiddling her hair with one index finger. "Did Marisol tell you anything after they questioned him?"

He shakes his head. "No, but I heard from a detective friend that Ketchum has no alibi for the time of the killing. Said he was out walking. Mrs. K confirmed it."

"That's bad," Donovan says, his slim eyebrows creased with worry.

"Yeah," Edward agrees.

"What about Mr. K spying on us?" Cassie has been wondering about that all night.

"His statement indicated he often does that on student films so he doesn't make the director nervous."

Donovan sits up like he got hit by an electrical jolt. "I'm sure that's true. He likes us to have…" He pauses a moment. "Autonomy. That's the word he uses."

Edward holds up his hands in a defensive posture. "I'm just telling you what I found out, and I probably said too much, but since you're both smack in the middle of this case, I think you need to be as informed as possible. On that, Detective Santiago and I are in agreement."

Cassie nods, happy that the two adults agree on something.

"I'm gonna crash now. Be careful this afternoon and I'll be cruising by at regular intervals tonight."

"We'll be careful, Dad," Cassie assures him, obtaining an affirming nod from Donovan. "Marisol—I mean Detective Santiago—said she'll have officers watching us shoot even during the day."

Her dad clearly notes her switch from "Marisol" to "Detective," but ignores it as he stands and gathers up all his gear. "See you both later."

He ambles out of the kitchen and Cassie hears his bedroom door close with a click. She and Donovan gaze at one another a long moment. She already knows his thoughts without asking.

"Asher *is* beautiful, which is why having him in the film is good for business, just like having Diego. You know that because we talked about attracting more female viewers. They'll love you too, by the way, but that doesn't make me jealous. Just because I think a boy is good looking doesn't mean I'm interested in him, Donovan. You of all people should know that. We're filmmakers."

"I do know," he admits, glancing down at the table and looking sheepish. "And you're right about Asher. He's photogenic as hell."

"Now that we have that settled, let's focus on this kill for tonight. It's our trickiest one yet."

She studies him for residual signs of jealousy, but doesn't see any. Oddly enough, she's slightly disappointed.

"Having no budget for special effects sucks," he mumbles.

They lean into their shot sheets once more, pulling over the corresponding storyboards and studying Donovan's remarkably detailed artwork depicting the death of Olivia's character.

Donovan loves the staging of William's backyard for the kill scene. It's bathed in a blueish glow from the kidney-shaped pool, its internal light spreading outward from the water like vapor from a cauldron. Two lights covered with blue gels and set on stands at strategic positions within the yard add a further unsettling ambiance.

Metal patio furniture with cushioned seats and a flowery umbrella adorn the paving stones beside the pool, and an enormous shade tree towers above the yard, it's sprawling branches thick with leaves. The key light illuminates the tree, creating grasping shadows that add to a sense of impending doom.

Diego stands by the tree looking annoyed as Olivia has one arm draped across his shoulders and gabs nonstop into his ear. Cassie is in the house helping William and Baxter practice the upcoming shot, while Donovan sits beside Kristen at the round umbrella table going over the scene, but also keeping watch on the Olivia drama from the corner of his eye.

Kristen turns yet again to glare at Olivia. "Can we just kill her already, for real?"

Donovan doesn't even glance over at Olivia and Diego this time. "We're almost there. We only have one shot at getting this kill scene right, so we can't screw it up."

Kristen growls like a dog. "We can't start soon enough for me."

Donovan sets down the shot sheet he's attempting to show her. "You know, she's just doing that to piss you off. I don't think Diego's interested in her."

Kristen snorts. It's almost a laugh, but not quite. "I know that better than anyone."

"Then don't let her get to you. You're super talented and if you're gonna make it in the industry, you can't let that kind of drama drag you down."

She loses her frightful look and sits back in her chair, brushing hair off her face and eyeing him as though she's never seen him before, or maybe as though she's seeing something new *in* him.

"I can see why everyone's so into you." And then she smiles. An actual, genuine smile, not one of her manufactured ones.

Donovan furrows his brows in confusion, his mind going blank with incomprehension.

What's she talking about?

When she says nothing more, but just stares with that revelatory expression on her face, he clears his throat awkwardly.

"Anyway, all I need from you, Asher, and Diego is to film her running out into the backyard. Once Jaden grabs her at that tree, you're done."

She resumes her all-business expression. "The kill will be the real one, by the copycat?"

"Yeah. That way we don't show the same scene twice."

After stabbing Olivia's character repeatedly, the killer hangs her from a large tree branch, which is their homage to Drew Barrymore's fate in *Scream*. *If* they can pull off the scene the way Donovan storyboarded it, of course.

Kristen glances over his shoulder and he turns to look. Jaden hovers by the big tree, cloak on, mask in hand, patiently awaiting his cue.

"It's weird how someone is doing the same thing to us that we're doing in the script," Kristen remarks, drawing his attention back to her. "Do you think it could be anyone on the crew?"

"You're thinking of Jaden?"

"You gotta admit he's spooky, always lurking around in that mask and staring at people. Including you, by the way."

Her dead-serious expression assures Donovan that she's not just being her usual condescending self. He considers her comment, then offers a very neutral answer.

"He is kind of odd."

Her lovely blue eyes widen to the size of boiled eggs. "Kind of? A regular Michael Myers if you ask me."

Donovan squirms, horrified at the idea that anyone in his cast or crew could be a murderer.

"Well, let's get this footage and then you can go." In an effort to distract her, he offers a smile he doesn't feel. "Unless you want to see Olivia die."

It works. She screws up her face in disgusted fury. "Oh, I do, but, unfortunately, I have to get home. Promised my parents I'd spend 'quality' time with them." She uses the air quotes with "quality."

Donovan can't remember the last time he had quality time with his mom, but brushes off that thought. "Okay. Let's do this."

She says, "I need to give my makeup a last check. Have to look good on camera, right?" and then tosses Donovan another sincere smile before heading into William's house through the sliding glass door.

Donovan notes Asher sitting in a deck chair scrolling through his phone and, recalling Cassie's mention of him spying on Warner, saunters over in the guise of prepping him for the scene, only to find him engrossed in what looks like a video.

"Hey, Asher, we're almost ready to shoot. You good?"

The curly haired boy looks up from his phone, a slightly startled look on his handsome face that quickly morphs into a beautiful smile.

"Absolutely."

Donovan thinks back to his conversation with Cassie and his flash of jealousy when she described Asher as beautiful. Gazing at the boy with this thought in mind, he sees the truth of her words. Asher *is* beautiful, with his sprawl of curly hair surrounding soft features, pale blue eyes, and that dazzlingly perfect smile—which is probably why his mother had him modeling.

He wonders if Asher was into the modeling thing or if his mom made him do it because she knew they'd make lots of money. The fact that he quit might indicate it was her idea. Whatever the reason, Asher looks amazing on camera. As a director-in-training, not to mention an artist, Donovan has no trouble recognizing beauty in both girls and boys because, well, in Hollywood, looking good on camera is often more important than one's acting ability.

But Asher has both—he's cute enough to attract female viewers, like Cassie said, *and* he's a good actor. But, for reasons of his own, he wants to be a director of photography when he enters the business. That's why he agreed to play the cameraman role in this movie, despite shooting a gorgeous-looking short film of his own for Mr. K's class. Maybe all that modeling turned him against being in front of the camera and inspired him to get behind it.

Donovan realizes his thoughts have wandered, and he focuses on Asher's phone, clutched tightly in the boy's small hands, noting the chewed fingernails. Asher usually comes across as laid back, but maybe that's all an act?.

"Anything interesting on the phone? Looked like you were watching a video."

Asher's hand slides over the phone to block it from view, but not before Donovan sees what he's sure is an image of Warner paused on the screen.

Asher tosses off that disarming grin that melts the hearts of so many girls at school. "Naw, just killing time. We ready?"

Donovan frowns. Asher *is* filming Warner. But why?

Realizing he hesitated in a suspicious way, Donovan smiles. "Yep. Kristen went inside to 'touch up' her makeup and then we're good to go." He flashes air quotes with "touch up."

Asher chuckles. "Girls are funny that way, always thinking makeup will make them prettier."

Donovan nods. "True, but the right makeup on camera is really important, even for guys. You know that, right? You're a cinematographer."

"Oh, yeah. But don't forget, makeup or no makeup, it's the lighting that's key to whether actors look good or bad."

Donovan realizes the truth of those words. As a director, he needs to remember that creating the right mood with lights is perhaps the most important aspect of setting up a scene. He grins.

"You're a DP, all right."

He holds up a hand and Asher slaps it.

As he heads into the house to consult with William, Donovan makes a mental note to tell Cassie about Asher watching the video of Warner. Could it be related to the murders?

True to her word, Kristen takes off immediately after filming her scene, along with Asher and Diego, and Donovan feels the tension on the set ease by a huge margin. With them gone, Olivia can focus on getting her "death" makeup just right—including a healthy splattering of blood-red Karo syrup on her face and clothes—and he can focus on staging the kill.

The tricky part, as he has known all along, is hanging her from the tree so it's safe, but looks believable. Preparation involves fitting her out with a full body harness beneath her clothes, which requires Cassie's assistance since the rest of the crew is male. The harness is one of their most expensive "props," but they had to splurge for it because—as much as Kristen would love to see Olivia get hurt—Donovan and Cassie must ensure the safety of every cast member. Plus, Mr. K had to sign off on its use.

The harness wraps around Olivia's upper thighs and waist, and thick straps travel up her back and over her shoulders to lock securely within the belt. There's a large ring at the top of the back straps that places all the tension at her core while hanging, but her acting and how she's positioned will create the illusion that she's dangling by the neck.

When Olivia walks out of the house in full makeup and covered in blood, Donovan breathes a sigh of relief that the fence around this yard conceals them from view of the neighbors. The police would be called for sure!

Complaining nonstop about her physical discomfort, she's finally attached to the thick tree branch by a rope that's run through the harness ring and secured to the branch. It takes Donovan, William, and Baxter some serious tweaking to arrange her so she looks like she's hanging by her neck and not her core, during which she spouts such encouragements as "Hurry up," and "If you idiots don't speed this up, I'll kick you where it counts," and Donovan's personal favorite, "Haven't you ever hung anyone before? Geez!"

Finally, she's secure. William uses the Steadicam and Baxter the drone to film Jaden appearing to hang her, complete with closeups of his hands and her face, which sports fake knife slashes. Once Donovan feels he's gotten all the coverage he needs, the boys unhook Olivia and help her to the ground. To show her gratitude, she shakes them off and turns to Donovan. "Let me see the footage. If you blew it…"

She doesn't finish her threat, but Donovan and Cassie exchange a shrug. They both know Olivia all too well after spending the last four years with her, so this behavior is nothing new. Her attitude makes Donovan doubt she'll ever make it big in the industry. Who'd want to work with her? Unlike Kristen, who can turn her attitude on and off at will, Olivia seems perpetually disgruntled.

They gather around the monitor to view the raw footage. Donovan feels quite satisfied and rather proud of himself. Once these shots are edited together, the scene will look as professional as any low-budget film he's ever seen, and better than many bigger budget ones.

"Whadda you think, Cass? Do we need to hang her again?"

Olivia snorts like a hog. "You better not! This Karo syrup is nasty."

Cassie ignores her. "I think we're good. William and Baxter caught everything, and you set it up perfectly. Good job, partner." She grins and offers him a high five.

He returns it with a loud *slap*. His pride in himself almost makes him forget the attack on his mother. Almost.

William turns to Olivia, wiping sweaty bangs off his forehead. "You can shower here, if you want."

She rears back as if she's been slapped. "Take a shower in your bathroom? Who knows what kind of germs I might pick up. I'll wash my face, change clothes, and go home."

Unfazed by her obnoxious attitude, William adds, "I could clean up the bathroom while you're changing in there, if you want."

Olivia's face twists into such fury that she looks like Medusa in attack mode.

Donovan blurts out, "Uh, good job, Olivia, and great work from the crew. I know that harness was tricky to get right, but it looked fantastic."

His diversion works. William and Baxter high five. Olivia loses her fury and gives them a smug smile.

"My drone stuff *is* great," Baxter gushes over a mouthful of foul-smelling chips. "Zoomed in on her face right when the rope choked the last bit of life out of her. Good acting, Olivia."

She lifts her chin like she's the queen of England. "Of course, it was. Now I'm going to change." She glares daggers at William. "Alone."

William exchanges a grin with Baxter.

Olivia glares daggers at Cassie. "Don't blow the finale." She spins and struts off into the house.

Baxter and William exchange a knowing look.

"Are we sorry to see her go?" William asks rhetorically.

Baxter opens his mouth to reply and William joins him as they both exclaim, "No!"

Laughing, they wander off to pack up the equipment. Donovan smiles as he watches them go. He loves his friends. They make filmmaking so much fun. He turns back to Cassie, only to find Jaden at his side. He jumps, his heartrate soaring into overdrive. Jaden's been so quiet Donovan forgot his was there.

"How was I, Donovan?"

Donovan catches his breath, embarrassed for being so jumpy, and studies Jaden's eager expression.

"You were great, as always, Jaden. Super creepy." He notes Jaden's smile slip and quickly adds, "I mean your acting, not you."

Jaden's smile returns. "I'll help 'em pack up." He jogs over to where William is loading the camera into its carrying case.

Donovan exchanges a guarded look with Cassie. He already knows her question before she asks it.

"Do you think the copycat will strike?"

Donovan pauses a moment to consider. "If he's trying to frame Mr. K, no. But if this is all just a sick game, then…"

She nods somberly.

The back door slides open and Marisol steps out. Wearing her usual business attire and severe expression, she crosses the well-cropped lawn to join them.

Cassie tenses up. "Anything strange out front, Detective?"

"No. Neighborhood's quiet. My officers are everywhere, parks, shadowy spots, anywhere we think someone could try to replicate your kill. If the copycat strikes, we'll be ready."

She sounds more confident than Donovan feels.

Cassie, always more assured than him, presses on, "How's Mr. K?"

Marisol's face gives the equivalent of a shrug. "I don't know. He's at Twin Towers and the deputies are keeping him under suicide watch."

Donovan's breath hitches in his throat. "Why?"

Marisol retains her professionally stoic expression, but the tone of her voice softens a hair.

"If he did kill that man in the park, which I doubt, remorse could take its toll. I've seen it happen."

Her words don't assuage Donovan's fear. "If nothing goes down tonight, what then?"

"Then you film your warehouse scenes. That's when the killer in your story is unmasked, so if anything else is going to happen, it'll happen then."

Donovan suddenly feels cold, even though the air is warm. This whole nightmare might come down to their finale, after all.

CHAPTER TEN

THE KILLER STRIKES AGAIN

O LIVIA, FACE CLEANED OF BLOOD and wearing baggy sweats and a tee shirt so as to not get residual Karo syrup on her designer jeans and blouse, enters her house in a much better frame of mind than when she left the shoot.

Donovan she can stand. He's kind of sexy in those fedora hats and mismatched clothes, but Cassie, and especially Kristen, are intolerable. Not to mention crazy Jaden and the pervert twins, William and Baxter. Geez! Who needs old man Warner around when she's got those two losers to fend off?

Of course, she thinks, as she flips the entry hall light switch, *there's always Diego.* He makes up for everything.

"I'm home," she calls out, suddenly realizing how quiet the house seems.

No one responds.

"Mom? Dad? Grant?"

No answer.

Confused, she makes her way down a short hall to the kitchen and flips on the overhead fluorescents. Flickering illumination becomes a full spread of light as she glances around. There's no sign of anything having been cooked on the shiny burnished stovetop, and there are no plates or bowls scattered around the pristine white counters. She spots a large sheet of notepaper dangling from a magnet on the fridge and snatches it off.

Noting her mother's flowing script, she reads: Olivia, we got a call that your grandmother went to the hospital, so we've gone over there. We'll let you know what's happening ASAP. Grant's with his girlfriend. Love, Mom.

Lowering the paper to her side, Olivia looks confused. Grandma was fine yesterday. Dropping the note atop the nearest counter, she slips her iPhone from her pocket and presses the side button for Siri. An incoming call pops up on her home screen accompanied by her hip hop ringtone and she gazes a moment at the number, not recognizing it. She presses the green button to open the call, placing the handset up to her ear.

"Hello?"

"Hello, Olivia," comes a robotic male voice, like someone is using a voice-changing device. "Did you enjoy dying tonight?"

Fear and fury invade her brain simultaneously. "Who is this?"

"Someone who's going to kill you for real."

Her heart lurches with fear, and then renewed anger floods through her as she realizes who this must be.

"Kristen, I know it's you, you sick bitch!"

She ends the call, trembling with rage. How dare that bitch threaten her! Her phone beeps for an incoming text. She slides it open and reads:

Your parents can't help you. I sent them on a wild goose chase. You're all alone.

Olivia's fury morphs into fear and she whirls around. Over one countertop she can see into the family room. It's dark, but appears to be empty. The house is dead silent. Gripping the phone tightly in her left hand, she eases her way out of the kitchen, flicking her gaze this way and that, then scurries into the family room, flipping on the light switch the second she reaches it.

The sixty-five-inch flat screen on the side wall reflects the room like a mirror. Couches and lounge chairs rest opposite the TV and the coffee table still features the Starbucks cup she left before heading off to the shoot. Directly across from where she stands, a sliding glass door leads out into the darkened backyard. She stares past the furniture into the yard, but nothing moves outside.

Her ringtone fills the room and she cries out in startled surprise. Holding the phone, she sees the same unknown number. Heart hammering in her chest, she touches the green button and opens the speaker mode.

"Kristen, this isn't funny!"

The robotic voice wafts out of the handset like a ghost. "Neither is trying to steal another girl's boyfriend."

Now she's sure it's Kristen and her temper flares again. "I was flirting with Diego because he's bored with you. Now stop this shit or I call the cops!"

She hangs up again, her breathing ragged with rage and fear. A *thunk* from behind causes her to wheel around. The hallway, just past the kitchen and leading to the rest of the house, is dark, but she's positive the sound came from somewhere down there.

"Is... is someone there?" Her voice quavers, despite her best efforts to keep it steady.

There's no answer.

Not even the creak of a floorboard.

Shoving the phone into the pocket of her sweats, she glances around, desperately searching for something to use as a weapon. She spots the large decorative blown-glass ball on the coffee table, a favorite item her mom bought on a family trip to Italy. She snatches it up and grips it tightly in her right hand, easing past the kitchen toward the hallway. The only sounds are her footsteps making the hardwood floor creak and groan. Easing herself forward, she raises the glass ball to shoulder height and flicks a switch, filling the hall with soft white light.

There's no one there.

She looks momentarily relieved until her phone rings again, startling her so much she baubles the glass ball, fumbling as it slips from her fingers. With a cry of alarm, she sweeps out her hands and cups them around the ball in midair, clutching it to her stomach in relief.

Her phone continues to ring.

Gripping the ball in one hand, with the other she pulls the phone from her pocket and gazes at the screen a long moment, weighing whether or not to answer. Then she opens the call with a touch of her thumb.

"I told you this isn't funny!" She tries to sound as forceful as she can, but hears the tremor in her voice.

"But we haven't even gotten to the good part yet," says the robot voice on the other end.

She backs out of the hall and returns to the family room, where she gazes across at the sliding glass door into the yard. If there is someone down the hall, the backyard might be her only escape route.

Battling a combination of terror and fury, she whips the phone back to her ear. "Screw you, Kristen!"

She hangs up and slides the phone back into her pocket. The lights suddenly go out, plunging the house into blackness. Shrieking, she drops the heavy globe and darts between the couch and chairs to the sliding glass door. She grapples with the latch, flicking terrified glances over her shoulder. She yanks the door open and pelts headlong into the darkness of the backyard.

Fumbling along the wall, she locates a light switch and flicks it. Nothing happens. She flips it up and down. Nothing! Petrified, she inches her way along the wall facing their egg-shaped swimming pool rimmed with fancy paving stones.

Reaching the corner of the house unmolested, she darts across the yard, scurrying along the tall wooden fence running parallel to the pool. Her eyes adjust to the darkness and she easily skirts the chaise lounge chairs and small tables. There's no sound except her sneakers slapping against the pavement.

She eyes her destination—a huge oak tree—on the opposite side of the pool, then breaks away from the fence in that direction. She's climbed this tree numerous times as a child and can easily access her neighbor's yard atop the thick branch extending over the fence. She just has to get *there* before whoever's in the house gets *her*.

Heart hammering, she quickens her pace, glancing around fearfully, but spots no movement of any kind. She nears the tree and breaks into a run, jumping up and grasping the lower branches. As she pulls herself upward onto the thickest limb, a hand closes around her dangling ankle and yanks hard. She screams and tumbles downward.

Olivia's parents step through the front door.

"Olivia, we're home!" Her mom flicks the switch, bathing the entryway in soft, warm light. She exchanges a glance with her husband when there's no answer to her call.

He scans the hallway leading to the back of the house, but no lights are on in any of the rooms. "She should've been back hours ago."

They walk past the kitchen. She sets her purse on the counter and surveys the stove and sink.

"Nothing's been touched here." Then she notices the note tossed haphazardly on the countertop near the fridge. "Well, she was here, unless Grant came home. Where do you suppose she could be?"

He shrugs, but doesn't look worried as he strolls into the family room and turns on the lights. Glancing around, he focuses on the coffee table, squinting as though trying to recall something. Then his eyebrows shoot up in surprise.

"That glass globe of yours is missing, honey. The one you bought in Italy last summer."

She enters the room and moves toward the coffee table. "That's weird. Maybe she needed it for a prop in the movie."

"Why is the sliding door open?"

His words draw her attention to the open sliding glass door. There's no breeze, but cool air wafts in from the backyard. "I don't know."

Together, they hurry out into the backyard. It's dark, though the interior pool light is on, filling the yard with a misty glow. He flicks a light switch on the wall beside him, and she screams in horror.

Alarmed, he looks out across the yard and gags.

Olivia, bloodied from countless knife wounds with a rope wrapped tightly around her twisted neck and her face a mottled dark blue, dangles from a thick tree branch at the far end of the yard.

She's dead.

Cassie sits hunched over her kitchen table across from Donovan staring at her phone screen as though willing it to answer her silent question: *Has anyone been killed yet?*

Donovan plunks down his own phone with a frustrated sigh. "It's almost midnight."

She studies his face. His normally gentle features are taut with anxiety and fear, making him look much older, especially since the fedora rests haphazardly atop his frizzy mop of hair.

"I know."

They've been plotting possible ways to trap the killer during the shooting of their finale and Cassie mulls over those ideas again while staring off into space.

"I don't think Asher is involved," she finally says after a lengthy pause, because his name has come up several times. "It's weird that he's filming Warner, but it's not like he's filming us or the crew. Didn't you say his mom loves Warner from those old movies?"

"That's what Mr. K said. Asher told me that, too."

"Depending on what happens tonight, why not just ask him what he's up to? You guys get along well."

Donovan nods. "Okay. I'll ask him tomorrow."

The front door opens and closes and, even though it's not loud, the sudden intrusion of sound into the stillness of the kitchen causes Cassie to jump slightly in her chair.

Donovan meets her gaze, his eyes wide and fearful as footsteps approach along the hall and then Edward appears, followed closely by Marisol. Both look disheartened.

Cassie leaps to her feet, heart pounding with dread. "Something happened. I can tell from your faces."

"Did someone get…? Donovan trails off, his voice tremulous.

Edward nods, looking like he's aged five years. "I'm afraid so. You'd better sit down, Cass."

Trembling from anticipation, Cassie lowers herself into her chair, her gaze never leaving her father's lined and weathered face.

"Was it another homeless person?" Donovan's voice penetrates Cassie's focus, but she doesn't take her eyes off the two adults.

Edward shakes his head.

Marisol wears her professional expression that says *I can't get personally involved*, but it's not quite so fixed in place as usual, like minute cracks have formed in a clay mask.

"I'm sorry to break this to you," she says, her tone somber, "but it was your classmate, Olivia."

Cassie's hand flies to her mouth before she can stop it, and Donovan gasps.

"Her parents called it in," Marisol continues, glancing from one of them to the other. "She was killed in her own backyard, which is why we didn't see a thing."

Cassie locks eyes with Donovan, and he says what she's thinking. "Same as our movie?"

"Yes."

Cassie feels like someone smashed a bottle over her head and the shards are digging into her scalp. The fact that she disliked Olivia adds fuel to the fire of her guilt. Donovan's devastated face is evidence enough to tell her that he feels even worse. She reaches out and clasps his hand in hers. He's so shocked he doesn't seem to notice.

Edward eyes Marisol. "So what now?"

Marisol studies Cassie and Donovan. "Anybody have it in for Olivia, that you know of?"

"Kristen," they announce simultaneously, but neither is amused at having done so.

Edward's eyebrows raise in surprise. "The snooty one?"

Donovan nods, his naturally olive skin devoid of color, making him look deathly ill.

"She's been fighting with Olivia the whole shoot," Cassie explains, keeping her voice steadier than her heart.

Marisol places both hands on the table and leans down with interest. "Over what?"

"Diego, uh, Kristen's uh, boyfriend," Donovan stammers. "Olivia's been, uh, hitting on him like crazy."

"But that's not a reason to kill someone, is it?" Cassie studies the faces of both adults.

Her dad and Marisol exchange a knowing glance that reeks of experience Cassie doesn't have.

It's Edward who answers her question. "You'd be surprised."

Donovan's phone, resting on the tabletop, lights up with an incoming text. He hesitates a moment before picking it up.

Cassie leans across the table. "Who's it from?"

Donovan's brows furrow. "Don't know this number." He opens the message and skims it, his pale face twisting into a look of panic.

Marisol darts around to his side of the table. "What?"

Numbly, he hands her the phone.

Marisol studies the message a moment before reading it aloud. "Don't even think of shutting down your film. That won't stop me, but it will get your mother killed. Those cops can't keep me from her."

She avoids Donovan's pleading gaze and focuses on Edward.

Edward whips out his phone. "I'll double the officers at the hospital. On your order, of course."

"Do it. And put a tracer on this number, though I'm sure it's another burner phone." She hands him Donovan's phone and he darts from the kitchen to make the calls.

Donovan looks so stricken with fear that Cassie slides her chair over and engulfs him in a tight hug. He wraps both arms around her like he'll never let go, knocking the fedora off his head.

"Dad and Marisol won't let anything happen to her." She forces as much assurance into her voice as possible.

"Like they stopped Olivia from getting killed?" His tortured voice sounds muffled with his head buried in her hair.

Marisol places a gentle hand on his shoulder. "Your mom is better protected in the hospital, especially with double the officers. This threat is just that, a threat to keep you filming."

Cassie meets her intense gaze. "Why?"

"I don't know. None of this makes sense. When did you last see Kristen?"

"She left right before we... killed Olivia." Cassie shoves aside the guilt that assails her.

"Diego too?"

"Yeah. They're always together. Why?"

Marisol hesitates, as though considering if she should speak or not. Edward steps back into the kitchen and she eyes him a moment before answering Cassie's question.

"The way we found Olivia hanging would indicate someone stronger than Kristen lifted her up there."

Donovan disentangles himself from Cassie, brushing thick black hair off his forehead. "But Diego's so mellow. I mean, he never even argues with anyone."

Cassie nods, realizing the truth of his words. "Yeah, it's almost like he wants to be invisible, which is tough with a guy that hot."

Marisol considers a long moment, again sharing a glance with Edward. "Tomorrow you're at the warehouse, correct?"

"Yes," Cassie answers, echoing Donovan's simultaneous "yes."

Marisol ignores their synchronicity. "Warner will be there. He has a sketchy past."

"Yeah," Cassie says, glancing at Donovan. "Dad told us."

Marisol eyes Edward, but remains silent. Her expression turns inward, and Cassie can almost see the gears in her head mulling over ideas.

"You have to keep filming; we know that much. Are there windows in that warehouse?"

"No," Donovan answers.

"Then the killer must be inside if he wants to watch the filming. I can have officers patrolling every inch of the place while you shoot."

Cassie meets Donovan's gaze and knows once again that they're on the same page.

"Wouldn't that just keep the killer away?" Donovan directs the question to Marisol, but glances Cassie's way. She understands what he's referring to—the ideas they discussed earlier.

Cassie directs her next question to Marisol. "This guy is following our story scene for scene, kill for kill, right?"

"It would appear that way." It's clear from her puzzled expression that the detective doesn't understand where Cassie is headed.

"Cass and I talked before you guys got here," Donovan says, his voice strong and resolute again. "If we're going to catch the killer, we need to flip the script."

CHAPTER ELEVEN

SHOOTING THE FINALE

K EEPING TODAY'S REVISED SCHEDULE FIRMLY in her mind, Cassie anxiously watches Donovan use a large key to unlock the back door to their warehouse location. Gathered around her are the minimal crew needed to shoot the finale: William, Baxter, Jaden, and Asher, who will assist William with the camera and lighting setups.

She glances behind her. The parking lot is deserted except for their cars. The immense loading docks are closed and locked and the lack of ambient noise increases her anxiety. The shiny white paint of the two-story metal exterior gleams in the bright morning light and the surrounding buildings—all industrial types like this one—slumber peacefully at the moment.

Having already explored the interior of this venue on a previous visit, she knows that the lack of windows will easily hide their activities from the world. The scary part is that same lack of windows will also cloak whatever the killer might try to do.

The door creaks as Donovan pulls it open and ushers her through, wearing a look of dread on his face. His thick hair pokes out from beneath his blue fedora and his unkempt clothes make him look like a load of tousled laundry. She understands. They talked late into the night with her dad and Marisol, plotting out today's agenda with meticulous precision.

The conclusions they reached as a group, coupled with worries over what unanticipated events might transpire in the course of the day, deprived them both of sleep—especially when they had to rise early for a Zoom call to cast and crew, outlining last-minute changes to the finale. Fortunately,

Marisol spoke to Warner in a separate call, for reasons she didn't articulate, but Cassie was all too happy *not* to have him in their group chat.

Everyone strolls past her single file, each person looking grimmer than the last. Her happy-go-lucky film crew are so beyond spooked at this point that she feels rotten, especially because of the revised schedule dropped into their laps only this morning.

Baxter munches on chips as he lugs the cumbersome box of sound equipment through the door, while William eyes her apprehensively from behind his thick brown bangs as he slips past cradling the camera like it's an infant. Asher carries the Steadicam and offers her an attempt at a smile, while Jaden brings up the rear carrying several light stands in his tight grip. He looks like he always does, indifferent and ready for anything.

Cassie enters last, giving the parking lot another quick sweep of her eyes. There's still nothing moving, not even a mouse. They have more props and lights to bring inside, but they'll get those once she decides on the best camera angles. She took tons of photos on her previous visit so Donovan could create the storyboards, but now that she's here in person, she must determine perspective, distance, and blocking. All in the two hours before her cast arrives.

Donovan flips on light switches beside the door, causing various sections of the cavernous warehouse to flicker into dim life. Since this place is supposed to be empty in the script, he doesn't flip every switch. Dark shadows loom all around them when the outside door closes, snuffing out the huge shaft of sunlight like a candle.

The interior of the warehouse is expansive and Cassie looks up and around at its vastness, eyes wide and alert. It's perfect for their finale, but unfortunately, it's also perfect for the killer to spy on them unseen. Catwalks crisscross each other overhead, allowing access to the upper floor that houses storage space and offices. Metal stairs at either end of the warehouse lead up to the second floor, and once Cassie decides on her camera set ups for the scenes that take place on the main floor, she'll head upstairs to scout the catwalks for the stalking sequences.

Knowing their time is limited, the crew, aided by Donovan and Cassie, set to work getting the camera and lights powered up and running. Baxter whistles while he works, something he doesn't normally do, and Cassie is certain it's to help him stay calm.

Once the basics are up and operational, Jaden and Asher remain on the first floor to assist Baxter, while Donovan and William accompany her up the old metal stairs to the catwalks above. No one speaks, which is weird on a film location, but the somberness of this day on the heels of Olivia's horrific murder has all of them on edge.

The stairs groan beneath their feet, but otherwise, the silence is oppressive. Arriving at the second floor, Cassie eyes the mostly darkened hallway to her right. The closed doors on either side are, if she recalls correctly, offices. Next she studies the metal catwalks stretching out from her position and crisscrossing above the main floor far below.

She has a clear view of the entire first floor through the slatted walkways at her feet and watches Baxter, Asher, and Jaden set up the prop table in the spot she'd selected. Picturing the camera angles she needs, she shrugs off her lingering fear to concentrate on the task at hand—shooting this finale as professionally as possible.

Once she focuses on the filmmaking portion of the day, time flies and she senses the same focus from Donovan and William as they help map out every shot from her hand-written sheet.

"Thanks for being so organized," William says, slipping his shot notebook back into the side pocket of his cargo pants.

She tries for a smile. "That's what preproduction's all about, right?"

He nods and they head back downstairs. As they cross the gray concrete floor to her first camera setup, Cassie leans in to Donovan and whispers, "You ready for the unexpected?"

He shrugs, but offers his shy little smile before whispering back, "That's not exactly possible, but yeah, I guess so."

"Me too."

They gaze a long moment at one another and she feels myriad emotions coursing through her, feelings about him and their future as a couple and what might happen today that could tragically end that possibility before it even begins.

Shaking off these worries, she heads toward the others, Donovan trailing like he so often does. She has to keep her head on straight and stay focused on the task at hand. *And* be ready for the "unexpected."

Piece of cake.

The cast arrives promptly at ten, and Cassie prepares herself for any questions they might have. They'd only been given the final pages yesterday, so they now know the identity of the killer.

At least, the one in the movie.

There isn't an excessive amount of dialogue in the finale, which consists of the unmasking and lots of stalking throughout the warehouse while lead character Ashley attempts to evade the killer.

Warner bubbles over, jubilant as he strides into the building behind Diego and Kristen. He struts up to Cassie and Donovan, grinning like the cat who'd just eaten the family parakeet.

"Finally, I shed my goody-goody teacher persona and show my true colors."

Donovan eyes his gleeful face distastefully. "I'm glad you're so happy to find out you're a serial killer, Mr. Warner."

Warner is already made-up for the cameras, including his slicked-back hair. When he cackles with delight, he sounds like the Wicked Witch of the West plotting how to get her claws on Dorothy.

"Ah, the villain is always the meatiest role to play. On stage, I portrayed Iago and Richard III. Of course, you children wouldn't know those characters."

Donovan smirks, indicating Cassie and himself. "Actually, Shakespeare is our favorite writer."

Warner's smug expression withers away. "Oh."

Cassie says, "Mr. Warner, William and Asher are going to shoot some atmosphere and cutaway shots right now, so why don't you rehearse with Kristen while we do our final preparations?"

His "cat that ate the parakeet" look springs back onto his face so fast it looks like a magician's trick. "With pleasure."

He makes a beeline for the scowling Kristen, who as always, has her makeup and character attire ready to go. He reaches out to take her arm, but she flashes a milk-curdling glower and brushes past him, striding across the vast warehouse floor to a spot away from the crew. Chuckling, Warner sidles after her. Asher stops assisting William and holds up his phone, filming Warner and Kristen as they meet up and begin rehearsing.

Cassie exchanges a look with Donovan.

"I'll talk to him," he assures her, glancing at Asher, who's oblivious to them as he records Warner and Kristen standing near the far wall running their lines. "We do have bigger problems to worry about, you know."

She nods. At least after today she'll be rid of Warner *and* Kristen. Asher, too, for that matter, though she does like *him*. Hopefully, none of them will be needed for later pickup shots. She leads the way toward William, who's filming in some dark corners near the stairs to use as cutaway shots to help build suspense.

He looks up as they approach. "Asher's supposed to be shooting this stuff, but he's acting weird."

"We know," Cassie and Donovan say simultaneously.

The overhead fluorescents suddenly wink out, plunging the entire building into total darkness. Cassie freezes, while Donovan sucks in a shocked breath. A few scattered emergency lights pop on throughout the main floor and high above the catwalks, but they provide only meager pools of illumination.

Cassie feels Donovan beside her, but can barely see him.

"What now?" His voice edges on fearful.

"A tripped circuit?" She spots his pale face floating in the gloom like a ghost, but can't read his expression.

"Nobody move," he calls out to the entire group, none of whom are visible, not even William who's only a few feet away. "I know where the breaker box is. Hang tight."

He rustles in his pocket and then a bright light momentarily blinds Cassie as he holds up his phone. He gives her a worried look that she fully understands. This is one of those unexpected moments that could mean any number of things.

"Be careful," she whispers, hoping her voice sounds calm.

"Always."

His phone light bounces across the warehouse floor and disappears through an open door.

She feels like her body is coiled into knots as she pulls out her phone and engages the flashlight. Trying her best not to tremble, she sweeps the beam around the area. It passes the prop table, but no one is there. As she moves it farther around the walls, she finds the crew huddled together fumbling with their phone lights. The three beams reveal Baxter, Diego, and

Jaden. Their faces look ghastly amidst the shadows, almost a horror film unto themselves.

She swings her light back to William behind her, who clutches the camera securely in his arms and makes no attempt to reach for his phone.

"What do you think happened, Cass?" He looks pallid against her bright light.

She hopes she sounds solid and brave. "Probably just a breaker, like Donovan said."

He nods, but doesn't look convinced.

Cassie sweeps her light in the direction of another illuminated phone and her beam settles on Kristen. She's alone.

Heart thumping, Cassie calls out, "Where's Warner?"

Kristen aims her phone light upward, casting garish shadows across her face and making her look like the murder victim, rather than the hero.

"I don't know. He wandered off in the dark."

Fear gripping her insides like a vise, she swings the light back toward Baxter's group. "You all right over there?"

Baxter illuminates his face, making him look like a bespectacled serial killer, and then briefly shines the light on Diego. "We're good, but Jaden disappeared. And no sign of Asher anywhere."

Another chill runs up her spine. "What?"

Panic squeezing the air from her lungs, she pulls her light away from Baxter and aims it at the door through which Donovan vanished. The door stands open and dark.

Be safe, Donovan…

Donovan allows the beam of light from his phone to cut a path through the pitch blackness of this narrow hallway. When he came this way that time Edward's security guard friend showed them around, it hadn't seemed nearly so far to the bank of panels that control the building's power supply. But then, the lights had been on and he hadn't been apprehensive about someone lunging out of the dark to attack him. He glances furtively from side to side even though all the doors appear to be closed.

But someone could be hiding behind one of them, his terrified brain whispers, causing him to quicken his pace past each wooden door as it looms up on him in the murk.

Could this blackout be the killer making his move or is it just a blown circuit like he told the others? Nerves jangling, he presses forward toward the wall of breakers at the very end of the hall. There's a pitch-black corridor branching off to his left as he nears the panels. Uneasily, he glances into that adjacent passage, but keeps his light focused ahead, so he sees nothing down there but darkness. Skirting a desk that presumably some maintenance worker used as an office space, he steps toward the panels.

Stabbing pain plunges through the back of his head and he staggers, dropping his phone and clutching the edge of the desk. Stars flicker in and out of his vision and he buckles. His knees slam hard against the concrete floor and he hears footsteps scurry away down the side corridor. In his stupor, he vaguely realizes he's been hit on the head before slumping into an unmoving heap.

Cassie stares through the blackness at the open door across the vast concrete floor, willing Donovan to reappear. How long has it been? Shouldn't he be back by now? When they went down there that day with her dad's friend, it hadn't seemed very far, had it?

What if something happens to him? What do I do then? I've never really told him how I—

Her thoughts freeze as a figure suddenly materializes out of the blackness at her side.

"Where's Donovan?"

She nearly screams aloud and clamps a hand over her mouth to stop herself. Heart pounding, she whirls to find Jaden's piercing brown eyes floating before her face.

"Don't sneak up on me like that, Jaden!"

He continues to stare. "Where's Donovan?"

She fights to maintain an air of self-control. "Uh, he went to turn on the lights. Through there." She points her flashlight beam across the way at the dark, open door and then eyes him suspiciously. "Where were you?"

"I'll find him." He sprints across the floor, his phone light bouncing up and down and disappearing through the doorway.

Cassie fights the urge to go after him. What if he *isn't* right in the head like everyone says? Donovan might need her help. But she fights her emotional impulses and stays with her crew. There's still the matter of Asher disappearing. And Warner.

There may be *much* more going on here than they planned for last night. She glances at the various phone lights scattered around the ground floor, but can make out no sign of Asher or Warner.

That can't be good.

Donovan's head swims in and out of consciousness, like he's rising and sinking in a pool of quicksand. He pushes up on one elbow and waits for his vision to clear. He realizes he's behind the desk, surrounded by darkness. A few feet away a lone beam of light shoots from his cell phone, striking the ceiling like a beacon.

I must've dropped it when I fell, his muddled brain realizes as he reaches up to grasp a drawer handle, noting that his crushed fedora rests on the floor beside his phone. Tugging to make sure the drawer is secure, he pulls hard while pressing upward with his other arm until he's on his knees. Throbbing pain at the back of his head forces him to pause so he won't collapse again. He waits until the spots floating before his eyes disappear and then, using the top edge of the desk, hauls himself to his feet, gripping it hard to keep from crumpling again.

His breathing steadies and he cautiously releases his tight grip on the desk just as a hand grabs his shoulder from behind. He cries out in surprise and whirls around, losing his footing in the process. As he starts to fall, strong arms wrap themselves around his torso and heft him back up, steadying him against the desk and allowing him to finally see a face in the dark.

"Jaden! Where did you come from? Is Cass all right?"

Jaden loosens his grip, but keeps his body pressed up against Donovan to prevent him from toppling again.

"Yeah."

When he just stares without saying another word, Donovan stammers, "Uh, somebody hit me. Didn't, uh, knock me out, but I've been stunned for a while, like somebody didn't want me turning on the lights too fast."

Jaden doesn't answer.

Feeling awkward with Jaden practically hugging him, *and* not speaking, Donovan mutters, "I, uh, I think I can walk now."

Jaden releases him. Donovan turns and takes a few steps toward the panel of switches on the wall. A wave of dizziness overwhelms him and he starts to sag. Those strong arms immediately encircle him from behind, gripping him like a vise and keeping him upright.

"I guess I spoke too soon." Wearing what he's certain is a sheepish look, Donovan glances back over his shoulder at the solemn face. "You're stronger than you look. No wonder you could push that dolly so easy."

Jaden wraps one of Donovan's arms over his shoulders and slides his other arm around Donovan's waist.

"Got me some weights at home. Come on, turn on the lights and let's get back."

Cassie blinks furiously at the sudden infusion of light when the overheads spring to life. Does that mean Donovan's okay? Once her vision clears, she stares a long moment at the open door, but when no one emerges, she scans the entire warehouse. Everyone is where they were when the lights went off except Warner and Asher. Warner stands by himself not far from the prop table and Asher loiters nearby, as though he'd been following the older man in the dark. She starts to look away, but then notices, a few feet behind the prop table, a door slightly ajar.

Was it open when we got here this morning?

She's heading to confront the smirking Warner when movement to her right distracts her. Jaden steps through the door he'd entered, now supporting Donovan, who holds his crushed fedora in one hand and looks unsteady. Fear stabs her heart, and she sprints to them.

"Donovan, are you hurt?"

She scans him up and down, looking for blood or other signs of injury.

"Somebody tried to knock him out," Jaden intones in his flat, sonorous voice.

Crew members and actors gather around as Kristen's sharp voice barks, "It was probably you, Jaden. You're the only one who went in there. Or maybe Asher. He was creeping around too."

Cassie glances at her a moment before facing Donovan again, her heart hammering. "Did you see anything?"

He shakes his head. "No, but Jaden helped me."

Now Warner joins the group, haughty as ever, sneering at Jaden.

"You could've knocked him out and then pretended to find him. Or this one could've done it." He indicates Asher who, Cassie has to admit, doesn't look entirely innocent. "He was following me, but I lost him in the dark."

Jaden's eyes flash with anger. "Why would I attack Donovan?"

"And I don't have any reason to, either," Asher puts in, his lovely blue eyes spitting pure hatred at Warner.

Diego pipes up. "I trust Asher more than I do you, Mr. Warner."

Cassie studies Warner's face, but he gives nothing away. "Where were you, Mr. Warner? You were supposed to be with Kristen."

He holds up a bottle of water she hadn't noticed and wiggles it back and forth. "I was thirsty. Went to the refreshment table. Is that a crime?"

Refusing to be cowed by his intimidating look, she meets his gaze a long moment before turning back to Donovan as Jaden releases him. Rubbing the back of his head, Donovan looks relieved to be standing on his own without help and gingerly replaces the smooshed fedora onto his head.

Jaden says quietly, "I'm gonna check the equipment to make sure nobody messed with it." Glaring at Warner, he marches away from the group.

Kristen looks at Cassie like she's crazy. "You trust him? He might mess with the equipment right now and cause some kind of 'accident' later." She uses air quotes for "accident."

Cassie and Donovan share a long look, clearly thinking along the same lines.

Donovan says, "William, Baxter, make sure you check everything carefully before we shoot."

They nod, but look rattled.

Asher looks offended. "What about me? You don't trust me to check for tampering?"

Donovan looks flustered. "No, it isn't that, but… well, they know the equipment better than even me and Cass, so it's better they do it."

Asher folds his arms across his chest in a huff and doesn't respond.

Warner smirks at him and if looks could kill, the one Asher tosses back at him would do the trick.

Cassie knows she needs to regain control now or she never will. Forcing down her fear, she addresses the group.

"William, Baxter, and Asher, as soon as the equipment's cleared for use, I need you all to grab your gear and head up to the catwalk for the unmasking scene. Kristen and Mr. Warner too."

Her commanding tone has the desired effect, because everyone scrambles to get ready. William and Baxter head for their equipment, followed by Asher, while Jaden circles the prop table, scrutinizing every item.

Cassie ignores Warner's intense stare as she awaits the result of the inspection. After a few tense minutes where no one speaks, William and Baxter flash her a thumbs up. Baxter grabs his drone, while William scoops up the camera and Asher the Steadicam.

"Okay, everyone," Cassie announces, relieved to be doing something productive, "let's head upstairs."

Feigning a calm she doesn't feel, she heads toward the nearest metal staircase. Kristen and Warner follow close behind, while William, Asher, and Baxter bring up the rear.

Jaden snatches up the boom mic and arcs around to where Donovan stands beside Diego. Confused, Donovan is about to speak when Jaden leans in and whispers something into his ear. Donovan flinches. Keeping his face as neutral as possible, he nods and Jaden heads for the stairs.

Diego catches Donovan's eye and raises his eyebrows. When Donovan shakes his head ever so slightly, Diego clearly gets the message, because he dons a facial expression a professional poker player would envy.

CHAPTER TWELVE
THE KILLER UNMASKED

FOR THE NEXT NINETY MINUTES, Cassie so loses herself in the artful world of filmmaking that she momentarily forgets the imminent danger they're all facing. The crisscrossing catwalks leading to dark and dingy storage areas on the second floor offer more stalking opportunities than she could've imagined. She's elected not to use many of the extra light stands the crew brought because she prefers the fluorescent ambiance. She knows those overheads will cast everything in a bluish tint on video, but she wants the otherworldly look it will create.

She puts Kristen and Warner through their paces as "Mr. Talbot," now wearing the black gown and skull mask, stalks "Ashley" throughout the upper floors. William captures the cat and mouse action from obtuse angles that should give the sequence a more gripping aspect. Asher shadows William and even dons the Steadicam to film some of the action so he can get an "Assistant Camera" credit on the film. Both boys incorporate a lot of Ashley's point of view as she searches for places to hide, and the upper floor has a seemingly endless series of nooks and crannies for both cameramen to utilize.

Cassie never gets so caught up in the action, however, that she doesn't scrutinize every area they enter for signs that the real killer might be lurking and spying, but there's no evidence of anyone but them.

Warner seems to take his job seriously, offering not a single leer or inappropriate comment. Cassie figures it's because of whatever Marisol said to him, but it's still a relief to have the filming proceed so smoothly. Kristen's acting is outstanding. She radiates fear and yet a fierce determination not to become the killer's next victim. As a director, Cassie couldn't be happier with the footage she's getting.

Finally satisfied that she has enough "stalking," she announces, "This stuff looks amazing. Thank you *so* much, actors and cameramen." She claps.

Kristen and Warner bow, while William and Asher grin like they just won the lottery.

"Now we shoot the unmasking, Kristen. We'll do the master first, so play out the entire scene."

Kristen wears her usual self-confident expression. "I'm ready."

Warner, mask in hand, eyes her. "As am I." He slips the mask over his head. In the dim lighting, it hovers like a bleached skull among intermittent pools of darkness.

"Places, everyone." Cassie moves to where the monitor sits atop a crate. Baxter supervises the sound recording, and Asher shadows Cassie because William will handle this scene by himself. She gives the curly-haired boy a smile, and he returns it, but his distrustful gaze quickly returns when he focuses on Warner.

I don't blame him, she thinks as she sits in a beach chair. *I don't trust Warner either.*

Kristen and Warner take their places on one of the wider catwalks, about ten paces from a railing that overlooks the concrete floor below. William moves into position wearing the Steadicam, adjusts the camera, and focuses on the two actors. Jaden holds the long boom mic and plants himself near William, but not so near that he'll impede the cameraman's movements. He lowers the end of the pole containing the microphone toward the actors, glancing at William as he does. William lifts up a hand to indicate "enough" and Jaden holds the mic steady in that final position.

Cassie checks the monitor screen. Kristen's face is framed in a closeup. "Roll camera."

Kristen instantly morphs from relaxed to terrified.

"Camera rolling," William announces. "Speed."

"Action."

Kristen, in full "Ashley" mode, lurches away from William as though he's the killer and backs fearfully toward the railing. Warner, as Talbot, casually strolls past William in pursuit, large knife up and ready. The blade glints in the dim lighting, giving the scene an even more ominous aspect. Cassie studies the monitor closely to make sure all the action is captured.

"Ashley" presses up against the railing, taking one quick glance over her shoulder at the drop. Petrified, she faces off against her masked attacker.

"Please, don't do this!" Her voice quavers.

"Talbot" approaches casually, knowing he has his prey exactly where he wants her.

"Ashley" leans back out over the railing, as though somehow it might help her escape him. But the catwalk isn't wide enough for her to get away. She's trapped.

He stops before her, eyes glinting malevolently through the holes in the mask. The skull's grin looks wicked in the dim lighting as the killer lifts his arm and brandishes the knife, preparing to plunge it into "Ashley's" torso.

"Please?" Her face quivers and she looks on the verge of tears, but the killer only chuckles.

Before the knife can move, "Ashley's" facial expression transforms in a split second from terrified to resolute and she snatches the mask off his head.

Startled, he takes a step back as she gasps, "Mr. Talbot!"

His disconcerted expression immediately shifts to one of amusement at her reaction. "In the flesh." He keeps the knife poised above her and doesn't appear at all troubled.

Still astonished, she asks, "Why? You were the best teacher ever."

"Remember what I taught you in class? In Hollywood, there's no such thing as bad publicity."

He sniggers, but her mouth drops open even farther. "You killed people for publicity?"

"Of course. Thanks to me, this film has garnered more publicity than it ever would've on its own. As a result, producers will break down the door to hire me. My past sins will be forgotten and I'll be back in front of the camera where I belong. You, dear Ashley, will be my final victim."

Her expression becomes feral. "Like hell!"

She punches out at his wrist, catching him off-guard and causing him to drop the knife, at the same time shoving him aside to run down the catwalk past William and the camera. Warner stoops to snatch up the knife and jogs after her, not bothering to retrieve the fallen mask.

"Cut!" Cassie steps away from the monitor as Kristen and Warner stop their forward movement. "That was awesome!"

She applauds, once again marveling at Kristen's acting ability. She's even been impressed by Warner during this shoot. If both of them got personality transplants, they'd be amazing to work with.

Warner bows while Kristen resumes her usual smugness.

"Of course it was," she says.

Cassie tosses William a thumbs up. "Great camera work. You totally followed the action."

William grins.

Cassie steps past him to the railing and looks down. Donovan has moved the prop table to the middle of the floor and laid out everything needed for the finale. He and Diego are speaking too quietly to be overheard.

"Everything ready down there, Donovan?"

Donovan looks up. "Yes." He exchanges a quick look with the silent Diego. "Uh, when you come down here, Cass, we'll meet in one of the offices to map out the final shots."

Even from this distance, she can see fear on his face. Has something happened while she's been upstairs? They already have everything mapped out so something must've changed. "Uh, sure. You set it up."

"Okay." He and Diego hurry across the concrete floor to an open door and disappear inside.

Strange, Cassie thinks. *He didn't even ask how the shoot was going.*

Fighting off the chill creeping up her spine, she turns back to her cast and crew.

"Okay, let's get the reverse of that master and then go for the closeups."

Another forty-five minutes passes before Cassie is satisfied that she has all the coverage and cutaways she might need in the editing room. She's probably shot *much* more than necessary, but its best to be prepared in case something doesn't cut together and she might need a closeup of the knife or the discarded mask on the catwalk to cut away to.

Everyone is effusively excited and looking forward to shooting the final confrontation between Ashley and Mr. Talbot on the ground floor. They bubble over with energy while tromping down the stairs, and Cassie absorbs that energy like an infusion of desperately needed sunlight. She'd managed to put the real killer out of her mind during the unmasking scene, but as she glances around in the dim light, her anxiety soars.

Is the killer here somewhere? She didn't see any signs that someone was upstairs while they were filming, not to mention they haven't shot a kill scene that can be copied. That's coming up in the finale.

What will happen after that, she wonders, but doesn't have time to give it more thought because Donovan stands in the open doorway to the office waving everyone over.

She has the sense he's employing his best acting skills as he casually asks how the footage turned out, likely because he's afraid the killer might be spying on them. She wonders about that too, as she prattles on about how great everything turned out. Once cast and crew are inside the somewhat cramped office space, Donovan closes the door, cutting them off from the prying eyes of anyone who might be in the building.

The office is, thankfully, empty, just a twelve by twelve room. William sets down the camera and Jaden leans the boom up against the wall, while Baxter holds his drone in one hand and binge munches from the bag of chips at his belt with the other.

Cassie holds up a hand to silence all the chatter and gazes firmly into Donovan's wide hazel eyes. "So, what's up?"

Her senses on heightened alert, Cassie gathers the cast and crew in the center of the main floor. All the regular props have been removed from the rectangular table except the two knives. Alongside them now rest a drill, screwdrivers, a wrench, wood glue and other items that give the impression this is a workstation for repairing various items.

William once again wears the Steadicam and adjusts the focus on his camera lens. Baxter twirls his glasses in one hand and continues his incessant chip munching with the other. Jaden wields the boom, ready whenever Cassie calls everyone to their places.

Kristen and Warner stand off to one side, appearing calm and collected and ready to step into their respective characters. Diego also hovers just off the "set," ready for "Pedro" to make his entrance.

Cassie and Donovan pretend to look over their shot sheets one final time, even though it's not necessary. She feels the tautness of his body as they lean in close to one another and must employ all her willpower to not reveal the fear coiled around her heart. She meets his eyes for a long look of shared understanding before facing the others.

"Okay, everyone, just like we laid it out in the office." She's pretty sure she sounds strong and focused. "Actors to your places." She glances at Baxter. "This will be the master shot, so no blood bags are needed. Those are for the closeups."

He nods, slipping his large glasses back into place and zipping up the fanny pack.

Warner grunts. "How wonderful. I so look forward to the blood."

Cassie studies him a moment, but sees no sign of him going against the new "script." In fact, he'd been the most eager to pursue it. Almost too eager.

Why?

He ushers Kristen into place and then takes up a position ten feet behind her. Shrugging off her worries for the moment, Cassie backs up and plants herself in front of the monitor, Donovan standing at her side.

"Roll camera."

William, camera aimed at the prop table, replies, "Camera rolling." He pauses. "Speed."

Cassie leans in closer. "Action."

Kristen, as "Ashley," instantly becomes "breathless," as though she's been running a marathon, and staggers in front of William's camera, lurching toward the prop table. She slams into it, breaking her stride with outstretched hands, and stumbles around it, placing the table between her and the camera.

Following close on her heels is Warner as the murderous "Talbot," waving the knife and laughing gleefully. He darts around the table in pursuit of "Ashley" and she backs away from him. William follows the action, capturing the scene from various directions to incorporate the best angles for each actor.

"Ashley" lunges for the table and snatches up one knife in her right hand, simultaneously grabbing the other in her left, thrusting them out in front of her with furious resolve.

"Don't come any closer or I'll gut you like a fish!"

She sucks in air, as though trying to recapture her breath, but holds herself strong and steady.

"Talbot" laughs mockingly. "Sweet little Ashley has some fight in her after all. Perfect. Shall we duel?"

He thrusts his knife outward across the table, but she leaps back and starts to run. Impressively agile, "Talbot" whips around the table in an instant and bears down on her.

She stretches out her left arm, prepared to skewer him when suddenly, from behind, she feels a hand on her shoulder.

Diego, as "Pedro," grins and says, "You two rehearsing—"

But he gets no further because the startled "Ashley," caught off guard by his presence, spins and plunges the knife into his stomach. His eyes bulge with shock and all he can do is groan.

"Pedro!" She gapes in disbelief as he crumples to the floor at her feet, the knife handle protruding from his midsection, blood pooling around him.

"Talbot" lunges forward. She spots the movement and whirls around just as he prepares to plunge his knife into her chest. She ducks down and drives her second knife into his stomach. He gags, eyes the size of golf balls as he offers one last look of astonishment before dropping in a heap onto the floor, blood spurting from where the knife blade lodges firmly in his midsection.

"Cut!" Cassie stands, looking furiously at Baxter. "Baxter, we said no blood this take!"

Stunned, Baxter turns to face her. "I didn't put any on them." He holds up two blood bags as proof.

Cassie and Donovan exchange a look of incredulity and then sprint over to Kristen, who stares, horrified, at the two crumpled bodies on either side of her. Thick pools of blood roll along the concrete from beneath them, staining the floor and seeping into the cracks.

Cassie finds herself frozen in place, so it's Donovan who squeamishly squats beside Diego to feel for a pulse. His hand trembles while everyone stares like a macabre exhibit at the wax museum. After what seems an eternity, he looks up, his face ashen, and shakes his head.

Cassie puts a hand to her mouth. "Oh, my God…"

She looks over at Asher, who has bent to examine Warner's prone form.

He looks like he's about to be nauseous and croaks out, "He's… he's, uh, he's dead. For real. This knife is… real."

Donovan stands, looking like he might faint, and points a shaking finger at the knife handle sticking out of Diego. "This one too."

Kristen looks horrified, her acting abandoned in the face of the unexpected. She backs away as everyone gazes open-mouthed and silent.

"Those were supposed to be prop knives. I didn't know…"

Jaden steps forward. "Somebody must've switched them when the lights went out. I thought something looked different."

Kristen gags. "Who would do that?"

Everyone stares at her, silent and reproachful.

"What? You think I did this? Jaden's the one who disappeared when the lights went out, not me." She juts out an accusatory finger at Jaden, but her arm trembles and she quickly lowers it.

"You hated Warner," Asher says, his voice timorous.

"So did you," Kristen flings back at him. "Don't think I didn't see those murderous looks you gave him every time he walked by."

"He didn't harass *me*," Asher replies, though he does look a little guilty.

"Yeah," Baxter pipes up, laying the blood bags back on the table. "We all saw you threaten him, Kristen."

"And you hated Olivia," William adds, sounding like the prosecutor on a TV show. "That was no secret."

Her face a mask of indignation, Kristen faces off against them. "You think I killed all these people because of Olivia? That's crazy!"

Donovan takes a step toward her, but she darts toward the table and snatches up a heavy wrench, brandishing it like a club.

"Stay back, all of you," she warns, her voice shaky. "Somebody framed me, can't you see that?"

The parking lot door flies open, splashing a wedge of sunlight onto the floor as Marisol, Edward, and five officers pour like water through the opening and surround them, guns drawn and pointed squarely at Kristen.

Marisol holds her weapon in a steady grip. "Drop the wrench, Kristen. Now."

Kristen shudders like she's freezing to death and looks around in terror at the guns fixed on her.

"But… I'm innocent!"

She stiffens, like she might consider making a run for it, but finally lowers the wrench and drops it to the floor where it lands with a loud clatter.

Marisol lowers her weapon and the other officers follow suit. She waves two of them over. "Cuff her."

Two of the cops scurry forward and flank Kristen, one of them slipping handcuffs around her wrists. She looks shell-shocked, a shattered version of her usually haughty self.

Marisol waves two officers over and points to the bodies on the floor. "Examine the victims for a pulse."

The female officer places two fingers on Diego's throat and then on his wrist, shaking her head.

The male officer crouches down beside Warner and examines him for signs of life. "He's dead."

Cassie hears sirens approaching and shakes off her stunned disbelief, turning to her dad.

"Dad, Marisol, what's going on?"

Her dad nods toward Marisol.

"As planned, we heard everything over the bugs we planted out here," Marisol begins, "which is why I called—"

She's interrupted by the arrival of two paramedics and more officers streaming through the open door from the parking lot.

"EMT's," she finishes.

Edward leads the paramedics to the victims while the other officers fan out to search the warehouse.

"I'm sorry we were too late to save them," Marisol says, looking more embarrassed than Cassie has ever seen her. "It all happened so fast and I was around the back interrogating a man loitering in the alley. Likely a decoy."

"But, you don't even seem surprised about Kristen," Cassie continues, indicating her classmate a few feet away. "Like you suspected her."

"We did, but we didn't expect her to commit a double murder right in front of everyone," Marisol explains, indicating the cast and crew. "Officer Stewart enquired among all your families this morning if anyone had ever dressed up as both Jason and Michael Myers for Halloween. Only one name came up." She indicates Kristen.

Kristen bristles, the old arrogance flashing in her narrowed eyes. "So, I like horror characters for Halloween. Why would I kill Diego?"

Marisol looks nonplussed, as always. "My best guess is he helped you commit the murders, especially Olivia's. Two people were needed to lift her up to that branch. He probably felt guilty and you silenced him."

"But I have no motive."

Edward steps closer to Cassie and fixes his intense gaze upon Kristen.

"Could be the motive in this very film you're shooting. Cassie always told me of your Lady Macbeth fixation. And your obsession with being famous. There's no such thing as bad publicity. Isn't that a line in the script?"

Cassie stares at him in horror. "You mean she did all this to increase her chances of making it big?"

Marisol shrugs. "Survivor of a serial killer attack? Talented young actress? Hollywood would eat it up, right?"

Cassie gazes at them, open-mouthed.

"She's, uh, she's right, Cass," Donovan says, his voice still shaky.

"This is crazy!" Kristen has the look of a cornered animal.

"I'd advise you not to say anything more, Kristen," Edward says, "but I'm not your lawyer."

Marisol tosses him an exasperated look as Kristen clearly recognizes the wisdom of his words and clams up.

Marisol waves at the two officers to either side of Kristen. "Take her away."

The officers escort the shattered Kristen past Cassie and Donovan to the door leading outside. In moments, she's gone.

Marisol turns to Edward. "Seal off this warehouse and get a forensics team here ASAP. The coroner too."

Edward nods. "Will do."

Marisol turns to Cassie and the others. "Okay, everyone, I need this building cleared. It's a crime scene. Leave everything as is except what you have on your person."

They stare at her, still in shock over what has transpired. Nobody moves.

Marisol claps her hands. It sounds like a gunshot in the quiet of the warehouse.

"You heard me, people, now." She waves over another officer, a tall young woman wearing a sympathetic expression. "Escort them out."

"Yes, Detective."

The young officer waits until Cassie and Donovan start zombie-walking toward the door. Jaden, William, Asher, and Baxter trudge after them, everyone looking like they're carrying the weight of the world on their shoulders. The female officer brings up the rear.

As she steps out into the bright afternoon sunlight, Cassie knows this is only the beginning of the end and steels herself for what's to come.

CHAPTER THIRTEEN

AFTERMATH

THE STUDENT PARKING LOT OF Performing Arts Academy High School is empty and forlorn as Cassie pulls into a space and parks. She takes a deep breath and expels it, pauses, and then exits the car. Looking around, she spots the unlocked gate into the school and heads in that direction.

It feels strange to be here alone, and once again she thinks how creepy an empty school really is—the perfect location for a horror film. Pushing open the gate, she steps through to the quad area and looks around for the custodial staff. They have to be here somewhere, but she doesn't spot any movement. The massive shade tree seems lonely without kids lounging on the grass beneath it and all the performing arts complexes look haunted. Of course, after what she's been through on this film, haunted buildings would be a welcome diversion.

The leaves on the tree's bushy branches waft in the gentle breeze and the effect calms her nerves. Her eyes fall on an open classroom door in the Film Building—Mr. Ketchum's—and she heads in that direction.

Stepping over the threshold, she pauses to look around in case the custodian is present, but the room is empty. Off to one side, several windows are pushed open, which helps the room feel less stuffy on this warm spring day. She notices the door into the storeroom is ajar and moves between the neat rows of empty desks toward it. Just as she reaches out to pull the door open, it swings wide and Mrs. Ketchum emerges clutching a large cardboard box.

"Cassie! You startled me."

"Oh, Mrs. K, I'm so glad to see you!"

Dressed in stylish pants and blouse with a light jacket open down the front, Mrs. K sets the box on a desk and faces Cassie in surprise.

"Shouldn't you be filming?"

Cassie leans against a desk. "Filming's over."

"What happened?"

"Mr. Warner's dead. And Diego."

Mrs. K's face collapses in shock. "What?"

Cassie lowers herself into a desk chair and struggles against impending tears. "Kristen's the killer."

Mrs. K leans against the heavy wooden teacher's desk, shaking her head in disbelief. "I can't believe it. I mean, I knew it wasn't my husband, but Kristen?"

"She switched out the prop knives for real ones, figuring we'd think Jaden did it. When we shot the scene, she stabbed them."

Mrs. K takes a long pause, considering this shocking news. "What became of her?"

"Arrested. My dad and Detective Santiago took her to the station."

"And where's Donovan? I hope he wasn't hurt." There's genuine concern in her voice.

"No. He went to the hospital to visit his mom."

Mrs. K steps closer and sits in the desk beside Cassie, placing a comforting arm around her shoulders.

"I'm so sorry, Cassie. I just can't believe Kristen… I mean, I knew she hated Olivia because of Diego, but to kill them both? Such bad form. And why Warner? He was a cad, at times, but a fun guy to hang out with. We had good times back in the olden days. He certainly didn't deserve a knife to the gut."

Cassie looks up, pulling away to study her face. "Bad form?"

"Pardon?" Mrs. K looks like she'd been interrupted while musing.

"You said it was bad form."

"Just an old expression. I think it comes from Peter Pan. I played Wendy when I was a girl."

"Was Kristen ever in that play?"

Mrs. K considers a moment, as though wondering why Cassie would be asking. "No. She told me all the plays she'd done before high school. Why is that important?"

Cassie pulls away and stands, putting a few feet between her and Mrs. K. "Donovan got a text from the killer threatening his mom. The killer used that expression."

Mrs. K shrugs nonchalantly. "A coincidence. Peter Pan is a popular play. Maybe I'm mistaken about Kristen."

Cassie studies her, noting how calm and collected the older woman appears, despite hearing the shocking news about Kristen and the others. "And how did you know Mr. Warner was stabbed in the gut?"

Mrs. K's mouth twitches ever so slightly. "It was in the script, of course."

Cassie takes another step back. "No, it wasn't. In the script, the killer got stabbed in the chest. Donovan and I changed it today."

Mrs. K shrugs again, but not quite so calmly this time, even looking a tad uncomfortable. "I suppose a gut shot seemed more realistic."

Cassie eyes her with a guarded expression. "I told Detective Santiago that I don't think Kristen could be the killer."

Mrs. K looks up at her, well-manicured hands clasped together on the burnished desktop. "Why not?"

Cassie pauses a moment, as though thinking, but she's really studying Mrs. K for any outward signs of emotion.

"She would obviously have had to get Diego to help her, which is why she would kill him to keep him quiet, but even if she wanted free publicity to boost her actor profile and even if she wanted Olivia and Warner dead, why would she frame Mr. K? She loves Mr. K. We all do."

Mrs. K looks nonplussed again. "I don't know. Perhaps she'll tell the police."

"She says she's innocent."

Mrs. K smirks knowingly. "They always do."

"Then there's Robert. The victim in his case was stabbed by somebody right-handed, but Robert's a lefty. Weird, huh?"

"Decidedly, unless he purposely used his left arm to misdirect the police. He's quite well built and undoubtedly strong in both arms."

Cassie isn't deterred by her logical assessment of the Robert anomaly.

"I also told my dad I remembered an old spear gun that might go with the arrow used in the first murder."

Her eyebrows shoot up in surprise. "Indeed? Remembered from where?"

Cassie focuses on her face, using her most casual tone. "Here. You brought it in three years ago to add to our prop collection. Said it was left over from an old underwater film you did. But you left the spear at home because it was too dangerous. Remember? I bet that spear gun is still with the props."

Mrs. K squirms slightly in her seat, her eyes flirting at the edge of discomfort.

"Can I look?" Cassie points toward the open door to the storeroom.

Mrs. K appears to consider the idea. "You said Donovan is at the hospital and your father is downtown?"

"Yes." Cassie studies her carefully, keeping her emotions in check.

Mrs. K waves a casual hand toward the storeroom. "By all means, take a look. I was clearing things out anyway. Even though my husband is innocent and will be released, the school's dumping him. Unlike Hollywood, they hate scandals."

"That's so wrong."

"That's the ed biz, my dear." She sounds casual, but looks wary.

Cassie steps past her and heads toward the storeroom behind the teacher desk. Mrs. Ketchum stands to follow, but reaches into the box she'd set down and lifts out a large old film camera.

Cassie notes the action from the corner of her eye, surmising that the camera must be heavy from the way the older woman grips tightly it in both hands. As Cassie nears the door, Mrs. K lunges forward and swings the camera.

Cassie leaps to one side and Mrs. K stumbles past her, the camera crashing down onto a desk. She keeps her balance as Cassie stares at her in horror.

"Why? Why do all this?"

Mrs. K stands tall and proud, every inch the movie star of old. "There's no such thing as bad publicity, remember?"

"So, everything was about you getting another shot at fame?"

Mrs. K grins, looking like the villains she used to play so effectively on stage and screen.

"Of course. My husband held that spear often enough, so I knew his fingerprints would be on it."

Cassie's dad has confronted evil of this magnitude over the years, but she never has, especially from someone she *thought* she knew.

"You'd commit murder just to be famous? And frame your own husband?"

Mrs. K gazes at her contemptuously. "You have no idea what it's like to live in the spotlight, to have everything at your beck and call, and then have it all taken away because of some stupid drunken escapades." She smirks. "Even though Kristen's been arrested, my husband will always be a suspect in the eyes of the media. And I will look like the loyal, victimized wife." She cackles jubilantly. "I'll be back in Hollywood faster than you can say *movie star*."

That laugh chills Cassie to the core of her soul. "You must be insane if think you can get away with this."

"I never killed anyone. Warner did it all. I even made sure his DNA was on the rope that hung Olivia."

Cassie begins to understand. "So, you did a Lady Macbeth number on Warner to get him to help you."

She grins. "Clever girl. And on red-herring Robert. I suggested he make a move on you and he did. When you rebuffed him, as I knew you would, leaving that costume and knife for him to find was a no-brainer."

"But you killed Warner. He was your partner."

"Correction. Kristen killed him. And now, there's no evidence linking me to the murders. Switching the knives made that part all too easy, especially because the double kill was already in your ever-so-helpful script."

Cassie presses on, determined to see this through. "Why frame Kristen?"

Mrs. K snorts with disgust. "Oh, please, she's the definition of the *B* word, as you kids like to say. A little prompting from me and Olivia was all over Diego, and Kristen knew he was cheating on her. Men are weak and easily manipulated if a woman knows what to do."

Cassie's mouth hangs open in disbelief. "You really *are* Lady Macbeth."

She gives a slight bow, but never takes her striking green eyes off Cassie for a moment.

"Thank you. It's unfortunate you remembered that old speargun. It doesn't directly connect me to the murders, but I'd still rather it didn't fall into police hands."

Cassie takes a step back, glancing side to side for a possible escape route. "So, uh, how will you explain my death?"

Mrs. K shrugs with that casualness that always made her such a difficult teacher to rattle.

"You were rummaging around in the storeroom and this heavy object fell on your head." She reaches out to grab the camera off the desk. "It's a solid old film camera. A tragic accident."

A deep male voice speaks from the open classroom door. "Now, now, Connie, we never talked about killing *her*."

Mrs. K whips her head around toward the door, her lower jaw drops open like a fish, and her eyes bulge with disbelief. "Impossible! I saw you die!"

Warner steps into the room, still in his costume and covered in blood, looking just as he had when Cassie left the warehouse.

"Perhaps I'm Banquo's ghost. Or perhaps I'm a better actor than you ever gave me credit for."

Mrs. K looks from Warner to Cassie in complete shock, and this time she isn't acting. "What is the meaning of this?"

Cassie doesn't smile, even though she feels intense relief that everything is almost over.

"We flipped the script on you, Mrs. K. The lights going off *did* freak us out because we didn't know what you were planning—especially after Mr. Warner hit Donovan over the head."

Warner looks at Cassie, a hangdog expression on his usually haughty face. "She said to slow him down. I didn't know what she was planning."

Cassie tosses him a look of disgust. "Obviously."

Kristen steps into the room, followed by a still-bloodied Diego, Jaden, Asher, Donovan, Edward, Marisol, and two officers. Mrs. Ketchum looks at them aghast, completely breaking from her typically stoic demeanor.

An unsmiling Jaden glares at her. "I knew exactly how I laid out all those props, Mrs. K, so I spotted the real knives right away."

Cassie's heart still pounds from Mrs. K's attempt to kill her—even though she expected something like it to occur—and fights to keep her demeanor steady.

"That's why we gathered together in that office before shooting the final scene, so you couldn't hear us," she explains, recalling Donovan telling her and the others about the switched knives. "We talked it over with Marisol, who was listening through this." She pulls out a small microphone attached to a wire from beneath her shirt. "And we revised our plan to use the knife switch to make Kristen look guilty."

"It was kind of a big rewrite," Donovan adds, "but it worked."

"You see, Mrs. Ketchum," Marisol explains, "Edward, Cassie, Donovan and I had a long confab last night about this case, and the six degrees of separation process led us to you, the one connecting thread. But the warehouse didn't afford us any cover and we knew you'd be inside somewhere. So we hid in surrounding buildings and listened in on Cassie's wire."

"We only had suspicions, Mrs. Ketchum, and no motive," Edward chimes in, "until the detective talked to Warner this morning. When he knew he was under suspicion too, he agreed to help, but we still needed hard evidence, so thank you for confessing to Cassie."

Mrs. K regains her aplomb, straightening her back and crossing her arms over her chest. "I'll denounce her as a liar."

Marisol doesn't look worried. "A faded Hollywood star with a history of drinking and drugs versus a teenage girl with a stellar reputation for honesty? I don't think so. Of course, there's always the video."

Mrs. K flinches, dropping her arms to her side. "What video?"

Marisol points to the bank of windows and Mrs. K whirls around. A drone hovers just outside one of the open windows, filming them. Baxter steps into full view, holding out his remote like it's the Holy Grail.

Mrs. Ketchum gasps in shock and visibly trembles. However, her instinctive acting skills slip right back into place and she turns her overconfident gaze onto Marisol.

"That video will be inadmissible in court. I didn't give you permission to film me."

Marisol points to the white board behind the teacher desk. "Yes, you did."

Mrs. K turns and stares a long moment at what's written in the upper right corner: Filming always permitted in this classroom. Beneath it are two signatures, *Mr. K* and *Mrs. K.*

Mrs. K visibly sags, like all the air has slipped from her puffed up conceit, but her green eyes still glitter with malice.

Kristen's lovely features contort in anguish, like she just lost her best friend. "Was I so horrible, Mrs. K, that you'd let me go to prison for life just so you could have your career back?"

Mrs. K tosses her a nasty look. "Yes."

Kristen recoils in shock, but Mrs. K clearly doesn't care. She faces off against Cassie and wears such a look of hatred that Cassie takes an involuntary step back.

"How did you know I'd be here?"

"That's my doing," Marisol says, stepping between them. "A quick call to the principal asking to have you come in and clear out your husband's stuff."

Mrs. K's eyes widen with comprehension, and she looks angry. "I wondered why he was so eager to have that done today." She tosses a venomous glower at Warner. "I suppose you'll spill your guts."

"You already did that, thank you very much. I only agreed to help trap you. But now I'll do whatever they want and hope I don't get the death penalty." He pauses a moment to pin her with a look of pure loathing. "All that talk about our future together. You played me like a fiddle."

Resigned to her fate, Mrs. K sighs dramatically, like she's reprising her Lady Macbeth role right then and there. "What's done is done."

Marisol waves over the two officers. "Cuff them both and read them their rights."

The two officers move into position behind Mrs. K and Warner, snapping handcuffs professionally around their wrists. Warner looks humiliated, but not Mrs. K.

As her acting teacher is led from the classroom, head held high and defiant, Cassie feels the weight of despondency that someone she trusted, someone she admired, turned out to have been such a fraud. It's like a huge chunk of her childhood leaves the room along with her teacher.

Asher defiantly steps forward and blocks Warner from leaving.

"What now?" Warner looks angry, in addition to disgraced. "You've been not-so-secretly filming me the entire shoot. Why?"

Asher's look of hatred mirrors the one Mrs. K directed at Cassie.

"You ruined my dad."

Cassie and Donovan gasp.

Warner is clearly caught off-guard. "And how might I have done that? I don't even know you."

"My father was Andrew Barton," Asher spits like a snake. "Does that ring a bell?"

Cassie has never seen this side of the normally gentle Asher.

Warner flinches, but clearly understands. "Ah, yes, my former limo driver. I'd heard he committed suicide. So sad."

"Because of you!" Asher practically clubs him over the head with his fury and clenches his fists like he might explode any moment. "You blamed him for that limo crash back when I was just a baby. You sent him to jail and ruined his life. He was never the same when he came home."

Warner shrugs. "Bad things happen, kid. Get used to it."

Asher smiles, but it's the nastiest smile Cassie's ever seen on him.

"I was filming you doing the same shit you did years ago because I wanted to disgrace you like you disgraced my dad, but this is even better, you going to prison. Hopefully, you'll get to share a room with my dad's old celly. I bet he'd *love* to meet you."

Suddenly, Warner doesn't look so smug. He pales as Edward steps forward and eases Asher away from the door.

"Come on, son, he's done for," Edward says, his voice gentle and soothing. "I'll do everything I can to make sure your dad's name is cleared."

Asher looks at him in such astonished gratitude that Cassie almost tears up.

Marisol waves to the officer. "Take him."

As he's led to the door, Warner flashes a fractured version of his movie-star grin. "You will put in a good word for me, won't you, my dear, seeing as how I willingly helped?"

Marisol gives him a stern look. "Yes, Mr. Warner, that was our deal. And it's Detective, never 'my dear.'"

He looks only slightly abashed as he passes through the door and out into the quad.

Marisol turns to take in the group, a look of pure admiration in her steely brown eyes.

"You kids were masterful. She must've taught you well because you sure fooled her. By the way, the man I interrogated said he saw someone in a baggy gray hoodie exiting the back door of the warehouse into that alley, so she was gone by the time we stormed the building. I need to get downtown, but Edward will stay and take your statements."

That last part catches Cassie off-guard. "Edward? Are you guys back together again?"

Marisol and Edward exchange a knowing look.

"We're working on it." Edward tosses off a shrug.

"More officers are on their way," Marisol says to Edward. "Secure this room as a crime scene and I'll need Baxter's drone. It's evidence."

Edward is all-business once more. "Yes, Detective."

She gives him a slight grin of amusement and hurries from the room, the clicking of her heels quickly fading away.

Edward studies the group before him. "You kids all right?"

Everyone nods. Their faces display equal parts pride over what they pulled off and shock at all they learned about Mrs. K and Warner.

"Thank you, Officer," Asher says quietly, his voice breaking slightly, "for helping my dad."

"In the end, Asher, a man's character is all he has," Edward tells him with genuine sincerity. "I hope your father getting his good name back can, in some small way, help you."

Asher wipes his eyes, looking embarrassed. "It will."

"Mrs. K was such an amazing teacher," Diego muses, shaking his head. "It's hard to believe she fooled us for so long."

Kristen nudges him. "You're an impressive actor yourself. You made her think you liked Olivia."

Jaden flinches. "We all thought you liked Olivia."

Diego eyes him a moment before exchanging a significant look with Kristen. Her face remains unchanged, but there's something in her eyes, a message to him to do what he feels is right.

He pauses a long moment and then says in his quiet voice, "Her motive of Kristen being jealous would never have worked anyway, because... I'm gay."

A ripple of shock vibrates through the room like an earthquake.

William flings the bangs away from his eyes, mouth dropping open in disbelief. "No way. You and Kristen have been, like, my relationship goal for the last two years."

Diego shrugs. "We're good actors."

"Diego's father is one of those super macho guys who hates gays," Kristen explains, holding Diego's hand supportively. "Diego knew I didn't want a boyfriend because that kind of drama could derail my career before it ever started, so we made a deal that worked out for both of us."

Cassie begins to see the bigger picture here, but before she can speak, Jaden asks, "Would your dad really kick you out if he knew?"

Diego's handsome face slips into one of true fear, not "acting" fear, but the real thing. "No, he'd kill me. Literally."

Cassie gapes in horror, eyeing Donovan, who looks equally stunned.

But Jaden doesn't look the least bit surprised. Instead, he nods with understanding. "So would mine."

Diego's look of grave danger switches to one of astonishment. "You mean, you're…"

Jaden nods, his features displaying trepidation. "I'm a good actor, too. Have to be the way my old man talks about queer people."

Donovan looks from one to the other, flummoxed. "I thought you were both crushing on Cass."

It comes into focus for Cassie at that moment, what she's sensed all along from both boys. "They've been crushing on you, D-Boy."

"What?"

Diego and Jaden nod, but from the surprised looks on their faces, it's obvious neither knew of the other's feelings.

Donovan looks flabbergasted. "When did you figure that out?"

"Just now," Cassie replies, finally acknowledging what she's suspected.

Donovan's cheeks bloom bright red and he looks down at the floor. "But I… I don't even… you know, *try* to be noticed."

Jaden smiles for the first time. "That's what makes you so hot."

Diego nods his agreement, and the boys who have more in common than they knew share a brief moment of solidarity.

Edward clears his throat. "Perhaps all this, uh personal drama, can take a back seat for the moment. I need to take everyone's statement, so gather out in the quad, and I'll call you in one by one." He turns to Jaden and

Diego. "If you boys are seriously afraid for your safety at home, we need to discuss that too."

"Yes, sir," they reply simultaneously, mortified at having spoken at the same time.

Two more officers enter with Baxter, who munches from a bag of chips. One of the officers holds the drone in his hand.

Baxter pushes his sagging glasses back up his nose while eyeing the awkward Jaden and Diego, and then Donovan looking like he wants to be anywhere but in that room. "Did I miss anything?"

Cassie clears her throat. "Uh, we'll fill you in outside."

Edward addresses the officers. "You men keep watch on these kids in the quad. I'm going to take statements until forensics arrives to seal the room."

"Yes, sir," replies the officer without the drone.

Edward waves the kids toward the door and they file out, all except Cassie and Donovan. Donovan shuffles his feet and looks uncomfortable, so Cassie nudges him. When he looks up, that shy little smile appears and her heart flutters with excitement.

"You two all right?" Edward scrutinizes them. "It's been a helluva week."

Cassie loses her smile as the weight of the past week suddenly descends upon her like a ton of lead. She eyes her dad in his full uniform, looking so serious and "official," yet still accessible, much the same way she used to see Mrs. K.

"Yeah." She pauses to think how to articulate her feelings. "It's just… hard to find out someone you trusted isn't who you thought they were."

Edward nods. "Yeah. That may be the toughest part about growing up."

Donovan eyes him with genuine concern. "Do you think you can make sure Diego and Jaden don't get hurt at home?"

"I'll do everything I can."

"And help Asher too?"

Edward places a hand on Donovan's shoulder. "I'll do my best, son. That's all I can do."

Cassie grabs her dad in a tight hug and presses her face against his chest. "Thank you, Dad, for being the best father anyone could ask for."

Donovan nods. "I second that."

Edward pulls him into the group hug and Donovan gratefully accepts it. Cassie relishes this quiet moment with the two people she loves most in this world and wishes it would never end.

CHAPTER FOURTEEN

A NEW BEGINNING

CASSIE SITS IN A RATTAN chair at the large umbrella table in her back yard, surrounded by her cast and crew. Donovan sits beside her, while the others relax on lawn chairs or chaise lounges. Everyone sips from tall, cold glasses of lemonade, and the bright, warm sun feels good on her face. Sitting here with her friends on a lovely spring day as if she hasn't a care in the world almost makes her believe she doesn't. But that's not true.

The media has been relentless the past day and a half, ever since the arrest of Mrs. K and Warner, with much of the story being revealed to the world. Donovan's mother came home from the hospital yesterday and she's also been inundated with interview requests about the attack on her. Being a private person, she's turned them all down. But that hasn't stopped the rabid dogs from pursuing Donovan. Or the rest of the cast and crew.

Cassie's dad provided a template for how all of them should handle the press. Since Mrs. K and Warner have only just been arrested and the trial will be many months in the future, the kids are to stick to the basic facts of the case and not offer any opinions, no matter how hard they are pressed by zealous reporters.

As to Asher, he was instructed by both Edward and Marisol not to upload any of his Warner videos until after the trial is over. Edward assured him that once the dust settles on this case, his father's name should be cleared of all charges relatively fast.

Everyone in the cast and crew, being accomplished actors, have no trouble handling the press. They acknowledge suspecting Mrs. K and

Warner of possible wrongdoing and agreeing to help the police trap them, but they don't know specific motives or how the entire scheme played out. By keeping specifics out of the press, Edward explained to them all, the prospective jury pool won't be tainted by details that should not come out until the trial.

Jaden takes a long swig of his lemonade and then interrupts the peaceful silence. "It's nice to get a break from all the reporters." He sets down his half-empty glass and glances around at the others.

Everyone nods.

"Yeah," Cassie agrees. "My dad's a good bodyguard."

Donovan wears the light blue fedora that's Cassie's favorite, short pants, and an ABBA tee shirt. He looks tired. "I think they got enough already to milk this story to death. Hopefully, they won't follow us around school next week."

Asher's handsome face clouds over. "Yeah."

Donovan studies him a moment. "You okay, Asher, now that Warner is finally locked up?"

"My mom is, and that's all I care about." He bites his lower lip and fiddles with his mop of curly hair. "I never told her Warner was on this film because I knew she'd freak. When it all came out, and she knew I was the one who asked Mr. K to hire him, she kind of blew up."

Cassie eyes him with concern. "Is she better now?"

He smiles for the first time today. "Yeah. She just lost it for a few, I guess 'cause he ruined our family and she hated him so much."

Donovan offers his shy smile. "I bet your dad would be proud of you."

Asher returns the smile. "Thanks, Donovan."

There's a long pause while everyone soaks up warmth and serenity.

William, looking pale in shorts and a tank top muses, "I wonder what will happen to the film class?"

"And our senior project," adds Baxter glumly, munching on his ever-present chips. He also wears shorts, but in his case it's a tacky flower-themed Hawaiian shirt covering his pudgy upper body.

Donovan glances around at the others, his face slipping into an expression of self-reproach. "Plus, Olivia's funeral is coming up. I know I shouldn't, but I feel guilty."

"You shouldn't," Diego says from his lawn chair a few feet away. He also wears a tank top and shorts, but unlike the other guys, he has the physique to make it work. "No way you could know Mrs. K was crazy."

Donovan meets his gaze. "I guess."

There's another long pause in which no one speaks.

Kristen, dressed in short shorts and a tight sports top that accentuate her dynamic figure says, "Well, at least we proved we could all work together, right, Cass?"

Feeling out of place in her long sweats and short sleeve shirt, Cassie nods at her, realizing the truth of those words. "True. Especially when it came to trapping Mrs. K. I wasn't sure we could pull it off."

Kristen shrugs. "With the level of acting talent in this group, there was never any doubt."

Donovan notices both Diego and Jaden staring at him and squirms.

"Uh, guys, I'm really not interested in dating anyone right now. That's something Cass and I have in common with Kristen. There's plenty of time for personal drama when we're established in our careers."

Kristen smirks at Cassie. "Like your dad and that detective?"

Cassie laughs. "Exactly."

"Works for me," Diego agrees. "At least till I move out."

"Yeah, me too," Jaden says. He gives Donovan and Cassie a long look. "You and Cass are, like, the perfect relationship goal. Flawless friendship with a chance of something more."

Asher raises his glass of lemonade. "I agree."

Cassie and Donovan exchange a significant look and she reaches out to take his hand in hers. "I take back what I said a few days ago."

He looks puzzled.

"You're not the third cutest. You're the first."

Her heart pounds excitedly as she soaks up the sight of his beautiful face and enchanting hazel eyes.

He blushes.

"You finally noticed what a hottie he is, eh, Cassie?" Kristen shakes her head with bemusement. "Took you long enough."

"Well… I've been busy," Cassie replies awkwardly, suddenly feeling like she's under a spotlight she wishes she hadn't turned on in front of everyone.

Donovan squeezes her hand. "You're the real star around here."

She grins, but before anyone can say more, there's a knock at the sliding glass door leading into the back yard. Cassie glances behind her and flinches at the sight of Robert hovering on the back porch. Donovan's grip on her hand stiffens a moment, but she squeezes it gently and lets go.

"Uh, your dad let me in, Cass," Robert says, looking and sounding nothing like the arrogant kid who kissed her less than a week ago. He's also not dressed to show off his muscles like he always did at school, but rather sports a baggy shirt and board shorts. His handsome face expresses remorse *and* humility.

Donovan scowls. "Robert."

Robert ignores Donovan's distasteful tone and focuses on Cassie. "He, uh, gave me a good talking to about how guys should treat girls. I never heard nothing like that at home. My old man's been making me hit on girls since I was ten. If I didn't, he called me names." He pauses, and then offers a genuine smile. "Your dad's cool."

Cassie and Donovan exchange a look. His momentary jealousy has vanished and, just as suddenly, she has a much clearer picture of Robert than ever before.

"You okay," Donovan says to Robert, his innate compassion rising to the surface, "after being locked up and all?"

Robert's face darkens. "It was *really* scary." He fixes his puppy-dog eyes on Cassie, shame filling them. "Anyway, I just came to say I'm sorry."

He turns to leave.

Before she can stop herself, Cassie calls out, "Robert."

He turns to face her once more, eyebrows raised as though expecting her to go off on him.

"Sit with us. We're just chilling." She indicates an empty chair beside Donovan.

His wary expression becomes a smile of gratitude. "Thanks."

He crosses the yard and plops down next to Donovan, who gives him the chin raise of approval.

Kristen claps her hands in a dramatic way to get everyone's attention. "Uh, people, focus here. Our movie is evidence in a crime and we can't touch it, but we still need a film to finish the class."

Cassie eyes her serious expression. "Mrs. K said Mr. K will be fired."

"He probably will be," Kristen agrees, as though that fact is of no importance to her. "But the class will go on with a sub and I want some dynamite footage for my acting reel." She tosses a glower at Cassie and Donovan. "You're the writers here. So, write!" She grins to assure them she's acting, rather than slipping into her old self-absorbed ways.

Cassie returns the grin. "Well, *supernatural* horror films are fun. They're hard to copycat."

William shakes his head. "Yeah, but they're hard to do on a super low budget."

Baxter takes a break from his chip-eating. "That's true."

The yard falls silent as everyone considers possible story ideas.

Finally, Jaden pipes up. "What about a cheapo monster movie, like what's on the Sci-Fi channel?"

Asher's face lights up. "Yeah, I could wear the rubber monster suit."

Jaden high fives him.

Donovan grins and holds up both hands in front of him like he's framing a shot. "I got it. An interdimensional flying shark attacks our high school."

Everyone laughs.

"I love it."

Cassie whirls around in her chair at the sound of Mr. K's voice. He stands just outside the door on the patio, dressed in long pants and a long-sleeved shirt, grinning unabashedly at the sight of them.

She leaps to her feet. "Mr. K!"

Donovan jumps up as Mr. K strides into their midst, and then everyone is up and surrounding him, chattering enthusiastically.

"Welcome back, Mr. K," Donovan gushes, his face alight with joy.

Kristen asks, "When did they let you out?"

"Yesterday." He looks apologetically at Robert. "I'm so sorry, Robert, for what my wife did to you."

Robert looks as happy as everyone else at seeing their teacher back among them and blows off the apology. "It's not your fault, Mr. K. Besides, now I've got all the *incarcerated-kid* roles locked up."

Kristen chuckles.

Mr. K looks older than he did just last week, his usually cheerful face weathered with stress.

Cassie can't imagine how traumatic this experience has been for him, especially spending time in county jail. From what her dad's told her, that place is worse than Hell itself.

"Well, she sure fooled me," Mr. K says, his voice low and introspective, as though speaking only to himself. "Always could. Probably always has."

He seems to emerge from his momentary reverie and suddenly realizes they are standing there staring at him.

"Anyway, that's not why I'm here," he goes on, back in the moment. "You're right that the class will go on, but I'll still be teaching it, at least till the end of the year. The school board declined to renew my contract given the negative publicity my continued presence might cause." He tosses off air quotes for the final sentence.

Cassie burns with anger. "That's so wrong."

"It is, but I've been getting calls from producers I used to work for. All this unwanted publicity reminded them that I was a pretty good director back in the day."

Donovan shakes his head in amazement. "So, Mrs. K was right. How weird is that?" He tosses a knowing glance at Cassie.

"Her attorney will plead insanity, of course," Mr. K goes on, his voice steadier than before, "so we'll see what happens."

Kristen frowns. "Maybe she was just obsessed with power, like Lady Macbeth." She shakes her head in disgust. "And I wanted to be just like her. Stupid me."

Mr. K places a comforting hand on her shoulder. "Don't beat yourself up, any of you." He removes his hand to take them all in. "Insane or obsessed, she was an outstanding actress. Anyway, now that my teaching career is sadly over, I've attached myself to a film project that starts preproduction in June. A horror film, oddly enough, about a serial killer in the South Bay."

The yard becomes a babble of excited chatter as everyone congratulates him.

"That's so awesome, Mr. K," Cassie gushes.

Baxter claps him on the back. "Fantastic."

Donovan grins. "You deserve it, Mr. K."

Kristen strikes a sexy pose. "Need a gorgeous actress?"

Diego grabs a seat cushion and chucks it at her. She ducks and sticks out her tongue.

Mr. K sports a smile as wide as his face. "As a matter of fact, I do. I need a whole crew. You're the most talented group I've ever taught and I want to hire you to work on my film."

"Really?" Cassie can't believe her ears.

"Really." Mr. K scans each of them in turn, like a loving parent reunited with his family. "The only consolation for losing my teaching career would be to continue working with all of you. So how about it?"

Cassie and Donovan don't even exchange a look. They simply exclaim, "We're in," causing an eruption of laughter from the others.

"Me too," Diego and Jaden say simultaneously. They look momentarily surprised, and then exchange a high five.

"Count us all in, Mr. K," Cassie asserts with a grin, perusing the faces of her best friends. "We're an awesome team, guys, and we'll take Hollywood by storm."

Donovan slams a fist into the palm of his hand. "Those suits'll never know what hit 'em."

Kristen chortles. "That's for sure."

William, Asher, Robert, and Baxter nod excitedly, the joy in their hearts reflected on their faces.

"I can't wait to work with all of you out in the real world," Mr. K says, his voice ripe with exhilaration. But then his face darkens and he tosses a mock glower at Cassie and Donovan. "But, right now, the fake world of school beckons. So, get to work on that script."

He flicks Donovan's fedora off his head with his fingertips and upends it, flipping it atop his own head, then grins rakishly.

Everyone laughs.

Cassie keeps her eyes fixed on Donovan with his moppy hair and kaleidoscope eyes. Their career is about to kick in, so it might be time to take their relationship to the next level. Will it be as predictable as plotting a screenplay? No way. But she knows one thing for sure—it'll be a lot more fun.

ABOUT THE AUTHOR

Michael J. Bowler is the award-winning author of *A Boy and His Dragon*, *A Matter of Time*, THE LANCE CHRONICLES (*Children of the Knight*, *Running Through A Dark Place*, *There Is No Fear*, *And The Children Shall Lead*, *Once Upon A Time In America*), *Spinner*, The Film Milieu Thriller Series (*I Know When You're Going To Die*, *The Horror Film Killer*), *Warrior Kids*, and *Like A Hero*.

His screenplay, "THE GOD MACHINE," won First Place in the 2017 Scriptapalooza competition.

He grew up in San Rafael, California, and majored in English and Theatre at Santa Clara University. He went on to earn a master's in film production from Loyola Marymount University, a teaching credential in English from LMU, and another master's in Special Education from Cal State University Dominguez Hills.

He worked producer, writer, and/or director on several ultra-low-budget horror films, including "Hell Spa," "Fatal Images," "Club Dead," and "Things II."

He taught high school in Hawthorne, California—both in general education and to students with learning disabilities—in subjects ranging from English and Strength Training to Algebra, Biology, and Yearbook.

He has been a volunteer Big Brother to eight different boys with the Catholic Big Brothers Big Sisters program, a decades-long volunteer within the juvenile justice system in Los Angeles, and is a single father to an adopted child.

He has been honored as Probation Volunteer of the Year, YMCA Volunteer of the Year, California Big Brother of the Year, and 2000 National Big Brother of the Year. The "National" honor allowed him and three of his Little Brothers to visit the White House and meet the president in the Oval Office.

His goal as an author is for teens and middle schoolers to experience empowerment and hope; to see themselves in his diverse characters; to read about kids who face real-life challenges; and to see how kids like them can remain decent people in an indecent world. As individuals, we're better off when we do what's right, not what's easy.

***

Website: michaeljbowler.com

FB: michaeljbowlerauthor

Twitter: @MichaelJBowler

tumblr: http://michaeljbowler.tumblr.com/

Pinterest: http://www.pinterest.com/michaelbowler/pins/

YouTube: https://www.youtube.com/channel/ UC2NXCPry4DDgJZOVDUxVtMw

Instagram: @michaeljbowler

Here's a preview of
THEY KNOW WHEN THE KILLER WILL STRIKE,
(which wraps up the storylines begun in *I Know When You're
Going To Die* and continued in *The Horror Film Killer*)

PROLOGUE

THEY SAT HUDDLED TOGETHER IN the darkest corner of a seedy smoke-filled lounge, finalizing their plans.

The loud voices all around ensured that no one overheard them.

"Just remember that you want to kill quite a few of the cast and crew. If even one or two 'accidents' happen, it will shut down the entire production, and you'll lose your chance."

"I know. What about your target? What's your plan?"

"That's my concern. You're the amateur here, remember? *I'm* advising you."

"I know. I was just wondering."

"Well don't. You have enough to worry about. After all, killing eight people during a film shoot is unprecedented. Everything must be perfect or some of them will slip through your fingers."

"They all deserve to die for what they did. And they will."

"That's the spirit. Now, let's go through the plan one more time and then get out of this hellhole. The smoke is killing me."

As the noisy patrons laughed and drank and surrounded them with foul-smelling smoke, the conspirators once more laid out their plot to commit mass murder.

CHAPTER ONE

I DON'T THINK IT WAS AN ACCIDENT

LEO SAT AT THE BOTTOM of the steps leading up to his expansive Victorian home, wondering if his mother's desire to fictionalize his brush with death at the hands of a serial killer might end up bringing real-world horrors back into his life. He knew his dread seemed crazy, and yet he couldn't shake the gut feeling that this movie was jinxed from the get-go. Still, he'd agreed—reluctantly—to be an advisor/consultant to appease his persistently pushy producer mother who, he knew, never would've stopped asking until he said yes. Fortunately, he wouldn't be alone on the set. His three—make that *only*—friends had also signed on in the same capacity, seeing as how they were fellow serial killer survivors and, like Leo, sought to ensure that their fictional alter egos were accurately portrayed on screen.

They all sat together on the steps awaiting the arrival of the actors who would portray them. That was another of his mom's "brilliant" (her own word) ideas: the actors portraying the four main protagonists would live with their real-world counterparts while the film was shot on location in La Costa, their small coastal town west of Los Angeles. Knowing his extreme shyness would pose a problem, Leo had objected, but his mother insisted, especially after she saw the actor portraying him.

"He's gorgeous, Leonardo," she'd gushed effusively. "Perfect for you."

Leo didn't even want to ask what she meant by that (though he was sure he knew), and he didn't have a chance anyway because she'd raved on about the pending production and how much fun it would be for them to work on something together for the first time in his seventeen years. She seemed to have forgotten that only a few months prior, he'd nearly died during the actual events she was now so eager to turn into the next hoped-for hit designed to generate box office gold.

Oh well, that was his mother.

"Aren't they supposed to be here by now?"

Leo glanced over at his best friend, J.C. Rivera, looking hot and uncomfortable in the designer shirt and pants he'd worn despite the eighty-plus degree July temperature surrounding him. Unlike J.C., who loved to show off his fancy clothes, Leo sported a plain tee shirt and old board shorts.

Blonde and petite Laura Benson, wearing a light summer shirt and shorts, glanced at her watch. "They still have five minutes, J.C."

J.C. grunted with disgust, causing Laura to toss Leo and Chet a grin. Leo had only met Laura that spring when she'd transferred to La Costa High, but she'd already proven to be a great and loyal friend, especially during those terrifying weeks when she, Leo, and J.C. sought the identity of the person who planned on murdering J.C.

Surfer blond Chet Hamilton, on the other hand, had been a bully most of Leo's life. Only his narrow escape from death at the hands of that same killer, and Leo's part in saving his life, had reformed Chet, folding him into their nonconformist group of oddballs who didn't fit the trendy, partying, self-absorbed mold of La Costa High School students.

Chet shrugged but said nothing as he relaxed beneath the warm sun in a tank top and board shorts. He used to arrogantly show off his ripped physique every chance he got, but that was before he'd nearly died. Leo knew he wasn't wearing the tank to impress the newcomers, but only because it was more comfortable in the hot summer weather.

"At least there won't be thirty-year-olds playing us teenagers like they usually do in movies," Laura commented, wiping perspiration from her lightly tanned forehead.

"I insisted on that," Leo commented dryly, "*and* those script changes I told you about."

"Thank God you got that garbage taken out of the script," J.C. spat, his handsome face twisted with anger. "I already get enough crap from my mom on that front."

"Me too," Leo agreed, noting Chet frowning beside him.

"I guess my part in the story couldn't be changed much," he said, his deep voice tinged with regret. "I don't know if I can relive what happened, and how I used to be."

Laura took his hand in hers and squeezed gently. "You don't have to be there when they're filming something painful, Chet. None of us do." She glanced at Leo. "Especially you, Leo, when they film the part where you almost died."

Despite the heat, Leo shuddered at the memory. "I guess. I'll take it one day at a time."

Laura offered a reassuring smile just as a black SUV rounded the corner and approached Leo's house.

Laura released Chet's hand and sat up. "Looks like they're here."

J.C. grunted, "'Bout time."

The SUV eased to a stop in front of the house. Leo and the others rose to greet their onscreen counterparts. Since his mother was the producer, Leo felt obligated to approach the newcomers first, despite his social anxiety screaming at him to run and hide. As he rounded the rear of the large vehicle, the driver's side rear door popped open, and out stepped a tall guy with sleek side-parted brown hair followed by a shorter guy with a thick head of curly hair. Leo started forward, but then whirled at the sound of screeching tires approaching from behind.

A dark sedan with tinted windows careened toward the two young men standing beside the SUV. They turned at the tire noise, but Leo was faster. He darted forward and tackled both guys toward the sidewalk. Just as they tumbled to the grass separating the sidewalk from the street, a smashing of metal against metal filled the air. Sprawled on the grass with the two guys beneath him, Leo saw from the corner of his eye the dark sedan speeding off down the street.

"Leo!"

Laura rushed forward, J.C. and Chet on her heels. They reached out to pull Leo to his feet and then helped up the young actors, who looked stunned but unhurt. The driver of their SUV leaped from the car and joined them, visibly shaken by the event. He was a young man, probably just a driver who worked for the studio.

"Are you guys all right?" The driver looked terrified, as though he might get blamed for this incident.

The shorter boy with the curly hair broke into an amazing smile that caught Leo's eye. He looked directly at Leo and said, "Yeah, thanks to Leo. You move fast."

Leo was so captivated by that smile he almost made eye contact but quickly looked away, confused by what had happened, and how this guy knew his name. "How…how do you know me?"

The curly-haired guy dusted himself off, while the taller one did the same. Leo found a hand sticking out for him to shake.

"I'm Asher King," the curly haired one said, his voice firm but not especially deep. "I'm playing you in the movie."

Leo shook his hand, still avoiding eye contact but thinking how much his mother's description of Asher fit the young actor. Just then he found himself surrounded by another guy—tall and Latino, wearing a tank top—and a gorgeous girl with shoulder-length blonde hair, dressed in stylish summer attire. Both looked horrified.

"Are you all right?" The girl leaned in like a doctor to examine Asher and the other guy whom Leo had tackled.

"Yeah, Kristen, we're good," said the broad-shouldered, short-haired guy. He faced Leo and stuck out his hand. "Thanks, Leo. I'm Robert."

Leo shook his hand and Chet stepped closer. "Oh, you're playing me. I'm Chet." He shook hands with Robert, who grinned.

"You're obviously Kristen." Laura offered a warm smile.

The long-haired blonde, looking relieved that no one had been hurt, shook her head in amazement. "You always greet visitors like this?"

Laura shrugged. "Only actors."

Kristen chuckled. "I think we'll get along just fine."

The tall, well-built Latino noted J.C. staring at him as though in awe and stuck out his hand. "And you're J.C. I'm Diego. I've been looking forward to meeting you."

Caught off guard, J.C. composed himself and shook hands. "You have, huh?"

Diego smiled, another photogenic show of pearly white teeth. "Sure. I'm hoping you can show me some dance moves during the shoot. I saw some of your vids on social media."

J.C. offered up a smile equal to Diego's. "You got it, man." He eyed Leo. "Here's a guy who knows good dancing when he sees it."

Leo glanced quickly away from Asher, who'd been staring at him the entire time, and gave J.C. a shove to the shoulder. Then he led the group around the front of the SUV where the young driver stared in hopeless abandon at the missing rear door.

"The studio'll kill me for this."

He sounded so morose; Leo placed a hand on his shoulder. "We got your back on this one."

"Yeah," the others chimed in.

"It wasn't your fault, Ron," Asher assured him in a gentle but firm voice. "We'll tell 'em what happened."

Diego sprinted on long legs into the middle of the street and retrieved the mangled rear door. Trotting to the back of the SUV, he waited as Robert lifted the hatchback, and then he slid the busted door into the storage space.

"For a small town, you have some crazy drivers," Kristen commented to Laura.

"I've only lived here about six months, but I've never seen anything like that."

"Me either, and I been here my whole life," J.C. put in, directing his comment to Diego, rather than the girls.

Diego and J.C. made momentary eye contact before Diego glanced down as though uncomfortable.

Robert stepped forward and grabbed two suitcases, one in each hand, from the back of the vehicle and set them on the asphalt. That caught Diego's attention and he grabbed a third. Before either boy could reach for the remaining baggage, Kristen darted forward and reached past them to pull out her two bags, both of which were larger than any of the others. Laura stepped forward to help.

"The boys have been razzing me for bringing two bags for only one week," she told Laura with a heavy sigh. "They just don't realize what it takes for us girls to look gorgeous, right, Laura?"

Laura chuckled but didn't comment. Leo knew Laura wasn't into fashion or makeup, relying instead on her natural beauty, which in his opinion was considerable. He tossed her a smile when Kristen wasn't looking, and she returned it.

Looking like he was headed for his own funeral, Ron, the youthful driver, waved goodbye to his charges. "I'll see you next week. If I'm still employed."

They all assured him he would be and, looking slightly less disheartened, Ron drove off in the SUV, leaving the the group behind on the curb.

"Well, this is definitely a strange way to meet," Kristen announced to the group, "but I, for one, am excited about this shoot." She faced Laura. "I can't wait to get to know you, Laura, and pick your brain for details."

Laura shrugged. "I'm not sure there's much in there to pick."

J.C. stifled a laugh as Kristen eyed Laura quizzically.

"We can head over to my house," Laura told Kristen, pointing at a two-door coup parked across the street. "Later, guys," she added, casting a look back at Leo and the others as she strode across the street. Caught off guard by Laura's abruptness, Kristen grabbed her two large suitcases to follow.

"I can help, Kristen," J.C. blurted, stepping forward with a grin on his face.

She gave him a stony look and he stopped. "I can handle my own bags, thank you." She hefted the bags and waddled across the street after Laura.

J.C. shrugged and turned back to the others. "Well, I tried."

"Kristen's kind of the antisocial type unless she needs something from you," Diego said with a shrug of his own. "I know her pretty well. Where's your house, J.C.? I love the retro feel to this neighborhood, all these old-school homes."

"I'm around the corner. My car is the blue Beemer just over there." He pointed at a shiny new BMW coupe parked in front of the Queen Anne-style house next to Leo's. "You ready to go?"

"You know it. I can't wait to start picking *your* brain." Diego grinned, and it was an infectious grin that Leo found quite appealing. So, apparently, did J.C., because he laughed.

"I think you and me'll get along great, Diego." He reached for Diego's large suitcase. "Let me help you with this." He grabbed the leather handle and tried to lift the bag, but it barely rose a few inches off the pavement before J.C. grunted and let it drop. "What you got in there, rocks?"

Diego laughed. "Naw, just a few dumbbells so I can keep up my workout."

J.C. glanced at Leo. "Another fitness nut like you, Leo."

Leo couldn't help but smile. Other than dancing, J.C. had never been into fitness.

Diego grabbed his bag with one hand and lifted it with ease. The short sleeve shirt he wore stretched at the biceps and prominent veins bulged on his forearm. "I'm ready, J.C."

Looking sheepish, J.C. waved for Diego to follow and started toward his parked car. "I'll check in later, Leo."

"Okay." Leo watched them a moment before turning to Chet, Robert, and Asher.

Robert eyed Chet's physique and grinned. "I bet you got some weights at your place, Chet."

"Oh yeah. I don't surf anymore, but I still work out."

"Awesome," Robert said. "I'll be your workout partner while I'm here."

"That'll be cool." Chet glanced at Leo. "I guess we'll head to my house. See you tomorrow, Leo."

"Later," Leo replied as Chet led Robert toward his shiny black Z4 parked just up the street. Then he turned to Asher, who was gazing at him intently. "Well, Asher, let's go in and I'll show you around."

Caught off guard staring, Asher quickly smiled and reached for his old leather suitcase. "Awesome."

Perturbed by the other boy's ogling, Leo led the way up the stairs toward his front door.

Cassie Stewart sat at on a barstool in her kitchen, sipping coffee and reviewing the call sheets for the first day of shooting. As assistant director to Mr. K, her job was to make certain everyone was where they needed to be throughout the shoot. Donovan Quinn, the love of her life, sat beside her, reviewing costuming and other details for his script supervisor role on the film. In many ways, his job was harder than hers because films were shot out of order, and he needed to keep track of every detail to make certain scenes or partial scenes shot on different days looked identical.

She glanced over at him, relishing the soft features, mop of brown hair stuffed beneath one of his signature fedoras, and his mismatched retro clothing choices. Donovan was one of a kind, and she loved him with all her heart. Feeling her intense stare, he looked up and smiled. She blew him a kiss and he blew one back. Then they returned to the work at hand.

This film, as yet untitled, was their first foray into Hollywood, thanks to their former teacher, Mr. Ketchum, who, when hired as director, chose Cassie and many of her graduating class as cast and crew. They were all excited to be working together on a professional project. She and Donovan never had a chance to finish the feature film last spring that was to be their high school graduation project because of the copycat killings that had occurred, killings based on those in their script. With that case wending its way slowly through the courts, their unfinished film was considered evidence and had been confiscated by the police. The entire experience had been devastating, especially for Donovan, who was more sensitive and in touch with his feelings than herself.

Cassie shoved these thoughts aside to focus on the project before her. This film was a fictionalized version of a real serial killer incident that had happened earlier in the year down in the South Bay. She knew that four of the surviving teens, including the one dubbed "Hero Boy" by the press, were consultants on the film, and she wondered how they would feel reliving their worst nightmare. She could relate somewhat, but these kids had almost died, and that was worse than what she went through.

"Hey, D-Boy."

Donovan looked up from his paperwork, perfect eyebrows raised questioningly. "What's up?"

"How do you think the others are doing, you know, meeting their real-life counterparts?"

Donovan shrugged. "I know Asher was super excited to meet Leo. I think he's almost nervous about playing him."

"From what the media said about him, Leo sounds pretty amazing. I'm looking forward to meeting him too."

"Yeah."

She paused to collect her thoughts. "Does it seem kind of, I don't know, heartless, maybe, to make a movie so soon after something horrific happened?"

He nodded, his face clouding over. "I agree. Kids died and Leo and the others almost did too. I don't think I could be part of this film if I was one of the victims."

"Mr. K talked to the survivors and their parents and assured them he would not try to make the story anything other than a fictionalized version of what happened."

"I know. It still feels…wrong."

"Leo's mother is the producer. It was her idea."

He grimaced. "Like I said, wrong."

"Do you think we'll get a credit for those rewrites we helped Mr. K with?"

"Doubtful. Writing credits require a certain percent of the script to have been written, and we didn't do that. Plus, we're not in the guild."

"Well, we changed the two boys' relationship from boyfriends to just friends. That took a lot of tinkering."

"I don't think it's enough." He paused. "I wonder why the producer wanted that changed. It worked for me."

"You heard Mr. K. The real Leo and J.C. aren't boyfriends, so this makes it more accurate."

"That's true, but this isn't a docudrama."

She considered a moment. "Maybe the boys objected. Since everyone who knows them will realize the film is based on them, I'd probably want that part changed too."

Donovan nodded. "That's true. Kind of makes you wonder what sort of mother would want the world to think her son is gay if he's not."

"Even if he is, it's not her business." She fell silent. Neither her dad nor Donovan's mom would ever do such a thing to them. While she disagreed with the timing of the film (so close to the actual events), it was a chance for her and Donovan to make their mark in Hollywood, and she trusted Mr. K more than any other adult except her dad. So, she overlooked the unsavory aspects.

"Mr. K'll make sure the shoot is as painless as possible for those kids."

He tossed off a small smile, which practically melted her heart. "For sure."

They kissed, pressing their lips gently together for a few lingering moments, before reluctantly returning to their work.

Here's Chapter One of my multi-award-wining first book in The Healer Chronicles, available at online retailers. Book 2 is coming soon.

MICHAEL J BOWLER

CHAPTER ONE

WHAT ARE YOU?

ALEX FIDGETED AS HE LAY in bed and listened to the wind outside. It had been an okay day at school – he'd only been called "Roller Boy" twice, which was almost a world record.

After school, he'd kicked it at Roy's house and they cranked *Hawthorne Heights* tunes and chilled. Even Jane hadn't bitched at him.

So why can't I sleep?

He didn't know the answer. His eyes returned to the dancing shadows that flitted across his floor from the window. His drapes were closed, but the wind whistled through the trees, and the shadows mesmerized him. The patterns of light and dark pulled on his eyelids, dragging him sunder. A dream loomed at the edges of his consciousness. One of *those* dreams. Sleep overcame him, and it began....

Ms. Ashley trudged down a flight of stairs from her second floor apartment, carrying several overflowing bags of trash. The traffic sounds were omnipresent, but otherwise the night was calm and clear.

A slight breeze ruffled her long brown hair as she slunk to the rear of the complex. Rounding the building, she passed alongside a sloping hill of ivy-covered ground toward the row of trashcans in the far corner.

Looking chilled and unsettled, Ms. Ashley lifted one lid and struggled to get all her bags in without spilling anything.

A rustling noise startled her and she whipped her head around.

The ivy-covered hill ascended upward into darkness, but there was no movement. Only a creepy silence.

She tossed her bags into the can and dropped the lid back in place with a hollow *clang*.

A large cat dropped onto the top of the can from somewhere above.

She uttered a startled cry and leaped back a few steps.

The cat meowed and she chuckled, extending one trembling hand.

The animal snuggled against it, wanting to be stroked. She ran her fingers through the fur around the cat's neck and under its chin.

More rustling leaves drew her attention to the ivy.

The darkness in this corner was deep and penetrating, with the vines and leaves snaking their way up the slope barely visible. Another cat materialized from beneath the thick cover of ivy.

Then another. And another.

In seconds, the hillside seethed with cats of all shapes and sizes. Their glowing eyes shone like eerie beacons in the night. The cat beneath Ms. Ashley's fingers hissed and swiped its claws at her, raking the top of her hand and drawing copious amounts of blood.

Startled, she cried out and yanked her hand back, gazing in shock at the dark liquid spilling onto the concrete at her feet.

Her body trembled with fear as she backed away.

The cats crouched on the hillside, poised and threatening.

The one she'd been petting wailed into the night, and then they were on her, leaping and clawing at her face and hair. Hundreds of cats streamed down the hillside and flung themselves at her while the big one sat and watched like a general commanding his troops.

Ms. Ashley screamed, but loud traffic sounds drowned out her cries. Flailing, she turned and stumbled along the side of the building toward the street, crying out for help.

Claws dug into her back and raked across her neck. Teeth sunk into her arm.

She shrieked in agony as they yanked out chunks of her hair and raked at her legs, shredding her sweat pants and digging into her

Her knees buckled, but Ms. Ashley managed to stay on her feet while stumbling headlong into the street at a frantic pace.

Suddenly aware that the truck was almost on her, she clutched at the nearest light post in desperation. One bloodied hand caught the post and slowed her momentum as the cats ceased their brutal attack. She gesticulated with her free hand, hoping to attract the attention of the driver. With her urgent gaze fixed on the truck, she didn't see the figure in black leap from behind the retaining wall right at her.

Strong hands pressed hard into her back and propelled her forward. The truck mowed her down in a splatter of blood and gore, flinging her broken body to the pavement and then crushing it beneath massive tires.

As the truck screeched to an ear-piercing halt near the corner, the figure in black melted into the darkness. Several cats sniffed the dead woman's remains before they, too, disappeared into the shadows. The first cat was the last to depart, watching as the horrified driver jumped from the truck cab and pelted toward Ms. Ashley's broken body.

The cat seemed to grin before vanishing into the night….

Alex screamed and bolted upright in bed, hair plastered to his sweat-sheened forehead. Heart thumping with urgent terror, he scanned his darkened room. The door leading outside was closed, but the ominous shadows still crept through the window. His desk was messy as usual, and the door to his bathroom stood ajar, but he'd left it that way. Everything looked like it had before he fell asleep.

Dropping onto his pillow, Alex fought to control his breathing and calm his pounding heart. God, he hated those dreams! Poor Ms. Ashley. He lay there, sweat making his t-shirt cling to his chest as his heart rate drew down. Could this dream be like the one about his parents? It seemed so real!

He lay in bed worrying about the morning, and what he'd find when he got to school.

Gradually, tree branches tapping against the house lulled him to sleep. The last image to assail him before he went under was that ugly- ass cat grinning at him before running off into the dark.

The following morning, Alex regarded himself in the bathroom mirror as he brushed his teeth. He'd showered and blow-dried his shoulder-length, choppy white-blond hair and it looked clean. People liked his blue eyes, when he didn't hide them behind his flowing bangs.

Alex finished pushing the brush up and down his teeth, and spat out the mint-flavored water, staring a moment at his soft, hairless cheeks and milky white skin. Sure, he seemed so innocent, a "sweet-faced boy," as his social workers had always described him to prospective foster parents. That's what made the whole thing worse. He *did* look like a nice kid. But no matter how hard he tried, he always screwed everything up. He always started spinning people. He couldn't help it. And once they figured out he was doing something weird, they got scared and wanted nothing more to do with him.

He'd already been through ten foster homes, and the only reason Jane kept him at this one was because she'd figured out what he could do.

"What are you?" he asked his reflection. As always, it didn't answer.

Jane Walters stood at the door with her ear pressed against it, while two boys sat at the kitchen table watching her.

Carlos, a burly high school junior, wolfed down his cereal, while freshman Juan glared with barely contained fury. Carlos grinned at the smaller boy. Juan flinched in fear and Carlos sniggered. Juan's cereal sat untouched in front of him as he reached with trembling fingers to touch his face, wincing at the pain. The left cheek and eye were black and blue and swelling rapidly.

A motorized sound came from behind the door, like a rising elevator.

Jane stepped away and jerked her thumb at Carlos. "You, out!"

Carlos's previous bravado with Juan dropped instantly. He swallowed his final mouthful and leapt from his chair. Snatching up a backpack from the floor, he bolted out the side door, never even glancing at Jane. She regarded the sullen Juan, folding her arms across her chest.

"You know what to do." Her tone left no room for argument. "What if he don't wanna this time? He said he wouldn't no more." "You know what'll happen to you if he won't," she snapped.

Juan nodded.

Jane observed her reflection in the large, ornately framed mirror, obviously looking pleased with what she saw.

She turned to him, practically pinning the petrified boy to his chair. "I'll be watching."

The motorized whirring s ground to a halt as Jane darted through the door into the hallway.

The door beside the rectangular dining table popped open and Alex rolled out in his wheelchair, wearing a *Hawthorne Heights* band t-shirt, black hoodie, skinny black jeans, his black and white high-top Converse shoes, and a backpack resting on his lap. He had Roy to thank for most of these clothes since Jane never spent a dime on him unless she had to.

He popped a small wheelie and shoved the door closed with a swipe of his hand, and then turned to Juan, whose head was bent toward his cereal bowl. Alex noted the behavior and frowned. It bothered him that he frightened Juan, but he didn't blame the kid. After all, he frightened almost everyone.

"Mornin', Juan," he offered in his most upbeat tone of voice as he dropped his backpack by the door. Was that upbeat? He so seldom felt that way he really didn't know what it sounded like.

"Hi, Alex."

Juan didn't look up. Alex noted the other bowl and half-filled glass of orange juice on the table, and frowned.

"Carlos must 'a heard me comin' and bailed, huh?" Juan said nothing.

Attempting to seem nonthreatening to the younger boy, Alex added, "Left his dishes this time. Jane'll be pissed."

Juan looked up, revealing his bruised face. "You mean 'Mom', right, Alex?"

Alex ignored the correction, gazing in shock at the other boy's battered face. Furious, he wheeled over to Juan. "Did she make Carlos—?"

Juan cut him off. "I fell, uh, hit the bed table. That's all."

He indicated the mirror on the wall with a slight head nod. Alex caught the movement and looked at Juan, blinking twice in response, his anger roiling.

Juan pleaded, "Alex, could you, you know…?"

His voice trailed off and he looked down at his cereal again. Alex scowled.

"I don't wanna go to school 'n look like this," Juan whispered, focusing his attention on the soggy corn flakes floating in his bowl like dead maggots.

Alex gazed long and hard at Juan. He was fourteen, but looked eleven or twelve, tiny and scrawny with brown skin, short hair, and big, fearful eyes. He wore baggy pants and baggy shirts, but they only highlighted how tiny he was. Had Alex ever seen the boy laugh or grin like a kid should? He didn't think so. But then, he didn't do those things either. How could they, living with a witch like Jane? He leaned in so Juan's head hid him from view of the mirror.

"You mean *she* don't want you to."

Juan's eyes looked round and filled with panic. "Please, Alex?" "Aren't you afraid, like the other times?"

He reached out to touch Juan's bruised cheek, but Juan recoiled even before Alex's fingers reached him.

Alex felt that punch to the gut sensation each time someone flinched from him, which was almost everyone, except for Roy and the kids in his class. "You *are* afraid. Guess I don' blame you."

Juan flushed red with embarrassment, turning his bruises a brighter shade of purple. "Alex, please?"

Alex sighed with resignation. His frown melted into a look of deep compassion as he brushed his bangs away from his eyes so Juan wouldn't be scared. At least, he didn't think he looked scary. The blue always seemed to calm people.

"Okay," Alex said, steeling himself for the pain to come. "Tell me."

Jane stood in a small closet directly behind the two-way mirror in the kitchen, smirking at the two men beside her. All the kids knew it was there, but they never knew when she might actually be on the other side. Another technique she'd developed to keep them in line. The men wore business suits, and one held a GoPro camera pointing through the glass at the two boys.

"Now watch real close," Jane admonished, though both men were already riveted to the drama playing out in the kitchen.

The younger of the two, Phil, watched intently, as though not surprised by what he was witnessing. As silver-haired Bob lifted the GoPro, his mouth dropped open in stunned disbelief.

Jane grinned as she turned from the boys to eye the two men. Shocked by what he saw, Bob lowered the camera and watched with his own eyes.

"You idiot, keep filming!" Jane snapped, her voice like a firecracker. Bob recovered from the initial surprise and whipped the camera up, continuing to record.

Phil's expression remained unreadable to Jane, but she didn't care.

These men were flunkies. The moneyman was all that mattered. "Wish we had audio," Phil muttered.

"You'll get it from the other camera," Jane said, directing his attention to the cupboard behind the boys. The door was ajar. From this angle, even through the two-way glass, she saw the blinking red light as it recorded.

Phil nodded while Jane watched, grinning at the stunned expressions of the two men beside her.

Through the mirror, she observed Alex spin his black magic, saw the pained expression on his face, and grinned when Juan, now uninjured, stared in wide-eyed fear at the freak beside him.

Yes, you're a freak, Alex, she thought, *but you're a freak who's going to make me rich.*

Alex's eyes remained closed, his features intent as his bruised face returned to normal. Several moments passed before his eyes fluttered open. "Man, Carlos—I mean that table—really hit you hard."

Juan had pulled away from Alex as far as his chair would allow. His eyes were wide and anxious, and his voice quavered. "Yeah. Well, I… uh, thanks."

He looked down at the table again, obviously afraid to meet Alex's gaze. Alex watched him sadly, and then glanced at the mirror. He scowled at his own reflection.

She was there, probably wearing that evil smile she had. Fighting down the temptation to flip his middle finger at her, Alex turned to Juan. "C'mon," he said with a heavy sigh. "We gonna be late for school."

He smiled as best he could manage, and Juan nodded. He rose from his chair and snatched his ratty backpack from the floor at his feet. Alex grabbed his own pack and rolled to the door, pulling it open. Juan skirted past him, making Alex feel like he had a horrible disease or something. He'd just helped the boy—for the seventh time already—and Juan was still afraid of him. But Juan's reaction was typical. Unless he spun them afterwards, everyone who saw what he could do pretty much freaked. He rolled outside and yanked the door shut behind him.

Inside the closet, Jane turned to Bob, who continued to run the GoPro even though the kitchen was empty.

"You can stop recording now," she said, folding her arms across her chest.

Bob suddenly realized there was nothing left to film and shut off the camera, staring at Jane with amazement. His face was ashen, as though he'd seen a ghost. Phil's eyes glittered with excitement, which Jane interpreted as astonishment at what he'd just seen.

"A million, remember," she insisted. "You tell him. Not a penny less."

Bob wiped his sweaty palms against his gray dress pants. "Oh, we'll definitely tell him, Ms. Walters. You can count on that."

Jane grinned.

Alex followed Juan along the side of the house. On their left rose a high, wood-slat fence separating Jane's property from her neighbor. He allowed his chair to roll itself down the sloping driveway past the five-foot hedge that took over for the fence and ended at the sidewalk.

Just as the boys reached the sidewalk, a little old lady stepped from behind the hedge and Alex nearly cried out with fright. The dream images of the night before had not fully retreated, and he realized he was more unnerved than he'd thought. Juan jumped like a frightened cat, but Alex knew why *he* was jittery. The stooped, white-haired old lady offered a toothy grin and held out a small brown bag to each boy.

Alex found himself grinning in return, and his racing heart settled into its normal rhythm. "Morning, Mrs. Rhodes."

She kept herself on her side of the hedge. "Mornin' Alex, Juan. I made you tuna today, plus my chocolate chip cookies."

Even though this was a daily ritual, Alex couldn't help but feel extreme gratitude every time. "Thanks, Mrs. Rhodes. I din' even get breakfast this morning." As though on cue, his stomach rumbled.

She glared a moment at Jane's house. "Doesn't surprise me." "*Gracias, señora*," Juan offered shyly.

Mrs. Rhodes smiled and turned away, observing Jane's house as she hobbled to her front porch. Alex noted that she was using a cane today, not something she normally did. Must be that arth-something or other that always bothered her, he realized. He'd spin her again as soon as he got a chance. She was always nice to him, and since she never figured out what he was doing, making her feel better was pretty easy.

While Bob and Jane discussed particulars of the pending deal, Phil wandered to the living room window and pulled aside the drapes. He observed the old lady hand lunch bags to the boys, and watched as Alex wheeled away down the street, the other kid following. Phil slipped out his phone and typed the following message: 'You were right.'

Alex didn't attempt to make conversation with Juan as they made their way toward school. Roy would be along any minute, but Juan would beg off and choose to walk. That's what happened every time Alex spun him.

Roy's F-150 truck rolled into view, and Alex couldn't help but feel good at the sight. Roy's dad had helped him buy the used pickup, and Roy worked all summer buying parts from junkyards and after-market places to soup up the engine and transmission. As far as Alex was concerned, Roy was a genius when it came to anything mechanical.

Roy dramatically honked the horn, as though the two boys couldn't see him right in front of them. It was their usual morning game and Alex chuckled like he always did. Roy pulled the pickup to the curb and hopped out. Alex barely had time to note Roy's skinny jeans, *30 Seconds to Mars* shirt, and shock of brown hair spilling across his face like an old mop before his friend bounded over and grabbed the back of the wheelchair.

Alex's chair was his one prized possession. A few years ago, when he'd had a cool social worker, he'd managed to get a super-sturdy chair built like the one a famous guy named Aaron used for his incredible stunts. Alex had only been seven when he'd seen on the news how fourteen- year-old Aaron mastered the world's first backflip in a wheelchair. It had amazed and empowered Alex to see someone who couldn't walk accomplishing something so spectacular.

His caseworker at the time, a lady named Sandy Quigley, had convinced the county to pay for his special chair on the grounds that it would be nearly indestructible and would not need to be replaced or repaired often. Alex had been so ecstatic he didn't even feel guilty for spinning Sandy into thinking he needed something like that.

Roy pushed Alex's chair around the front of the truck to the passenger side and yanked open the door. Alex tossed his backpack onto the floor as Roy extended his arms and grinned. The double piercings at each side of his lower lip glinted in the morning sun. Alex smiled and slid forward, allowing Roy to sweep him up and toss him onto the passenger seat, grunting as he did.

"Getting too buff, Alex," Roy said. "You should be tossing me into the car."

"Yer just mad cuz I'm younger and can beat yer ass at arm wrestling," Alex retorted as Roy grinned and slammed the door.

Roy grabbed the chair, popped out the cushion, folded it into itself and slipped both chair and cushion up and into the bed of his pickup. He noticed Juan walking away in the direction of Mark Twain and called out. "Hey, Juan, doncha wanna ride?"

Juan turned and shook his head. "Not today, Roy. Thanks." He hurried away, as though trying to put as much distance between himself and Alex as possible.

Alex watched through the rearview as his housemate scurried away like a frightened rabbit.

Roy climbed into the cab and slammed his door, flipping his ragged bangs off his face and jerking a thumb behind him. "'Sup with him today?"

Alex shrugged. "Jane had Carlos beat him up so I hadda spin 'im. You know how he trips."

Roy cast a disgusted look Alex's way. "I hate that bitch. You need to spin her but good."

Alex tried for a smile, but those horrific dream images returned in force.

"Don't tempt me."

When Roy didn't start the engine right away, Alex looked at him through his surfer-white bangs. "We're gonna be late."

Roy shrugged. He wore the black Levi's jacket Alex loved, the one with the rips in it that looked so cool. If Roy wasn't Special Ed like him, he'd be one of the sickest kids on campus.

Roy reached down to the floor beneath his seat and pulled out a small package wrapped in black paper. "Happy birthday, fool." He tossed Alex the box.

Oh, crap! Alex thought as he fumbled to catch the box that fell into his lap. He'd completely forgotten! What with his latest nightmare and having to spin Juan, his fifteenth birthday never even crossed his mind. Blushing and making his pale skin look like a tomato, Alex grinned.

"Thanks, man. I forgot."

Roy shoved his bangs aside again. "I didn't. Open it."

Almost giddy at receiving a real present, Alex tore off the paper with gusto, and gaped at what he found underneath. A Nexus phone, still in the box. Brand new!

His chest tightened, like the wind had been knocked from his lungs. Other than his wheelchair, he'd never been given anything this nice since he was four. He looked at the grinning Roy with open-mouthed astonishment. "Oh, man, Roy, I dunno what to say."

Roy laughed, a rarity for him. "How 'bout, thanks, Roy, for being my awesomest friend."

"Thanks, Roy, for being my *most* awesomest friend. But, this is too much, man. And I got no money for a plan. You know how Jane–"

"Screw her!" Roy spat. "You know I make money fixing engines and stuff and my dad let me put you on our plan. He hates that bitch as much as I do."

Alex felt funny, like he was taking advantage of Roy. "I never had a phone before…."

"It's time you did," Roy said, grabbing the box and ripping off the plastic covering. As he opened the box and slid out the smartphone, he added,

"Now you can call me any time. I know we can't text a lot, but I'll put apps on it so we can see each other when we talk."

Alex grinned. Jane never let the boys use her house phone, and she didn't allow them to have cell phones, either. The others were on probation and she'd convinced their probation officers that "Cell phones are an invitation to trouble."

"I gotta hide this from Jane," Alex said, his face clouding over. "She'll take it away."

"Over my dead body."

Alex loved how protective Roy was of him.

"Thanks, Roy," he said shyly, gazing in awe at the bright, crystal clear home screen. *His own phone! Wow!*

"We better get to school," Roy said, turning the ignition. "You know how Ms. Ashley gets when we're late."

The mention of Ms. Ashley pushed aside all the joy he felt at receiving Roy's gift, and flooded his mind with bloodied images of her demise in his dream. He shivered, seeing once more the face of that huge, grinning cat.

"Yeah, let's get going."

Suddenly, he wanted to get to school. But he feared it, too, because deep down he knew his teacher wouldn't be there today, or any of the days to come.

Roy made a U-turn and pulled out into the quiet residential street toward Mark Twain High.